Copyright Matthew Cash
Edited by Linda Nagle.
All rights reserved. No reproduced in any form or by any means, except by inclusion of brief quotations in a review, without permission in writing from the publisher.

This book is a work of fiction. The characters and situations in this book are imaginary. No resemblance is intended between these characters and any persons, living or dead.

This book is sold subject to the condition that it shall not, by way of trade or otherwise, be lent, resold, hired out or otherwise circulated without the publisher's prior consent in any form of binding or cover other than that in which it is published and without a similar condition including this condition being imposed on the subsequent purchaser.

Contains excerpts from the poem 'Connected to You' by Paul B Morris.

Published in Great Britain in 2021 by Matthew Cash/ Burdizzo Books Walsall, UK

Your Frightful Spirit Stayed

Your Frightful Spirit Stayed

Matthew Cash

Burdizzo Books 2021

Last Christmas

What's being said is not a lie,
I'm still afraid to hold up the mirror,
its reflection resonates a pain within,
After all these years, I cannot help but cry.

Your Frightful Spirit Stayed

1.

Everything's a donation, from the furniture he sits on, to the coins that jangle in his pocket. Charlie gets money from the government once a fortnight; he doesn't know what it's called, doesn't care, just as long as they keep paying.

The flat they've given him is dry and cold but there's a sofa and an old mattress, so he has all he needs. Charlie knows he will find himself again once he has acclimatised to the outside world.

A clatter from the spare room brings him from his daze. "What the fucking hell is that?"

Words are harder to pronounce without front teeth, but Duncan understands.

The thin, wiry man stands with his back to him, taking in the view, a shadow against the sky, the balcony railing just visible through his spine. "Why don't you go and have a butcher's?"

Charlie pushes off his heavy coat and rises from the sunken settee with great difficulty.

He aged so much in jail, inside and out.

Near-crippling pain shoots up his right hip and lower back, so he hangs over the coffee table until the hurt fades.

He lifts empty lager cans whilst he's bent, gleaning for dregs. They are all dry.

"You'll get more when you're out," Duncan says slowly, and winks at him with his sole remaining eye.

Charlie swears as he straightens up and walks stiffly from the lounge to the spare bedroom.

The door is half bare wood, half painted with a translucent layer of undercoat. Six bolts are crudely screwed to the door and the post at random intervals. Charlie stares at them as though he has never seen them in his life.

Inside the room comes the sound of a boy crying.

"You going to stay with him whilst I ring the security in the centre, Charlie?"

Charlie turns.

It's Michelle, with her long straw-berry blonde hair and nose piercing.

"Yeah," he says after a fashion, "can't have them bastards nicking off us all the time. I'll hold him 'til the guards get here." He puts his ear to the door and can hear the shoplifting wanker yelling profanities.

Charlie grabs his coat; it's cold outside and he needs more booze.

2.

Red.
Red legs.

Charlie looks down at a cheap, felt Santa suit covered in dried vomit. It takes him far too long to realise the body inside it is his.

"Look at the fucking state of you," Duncan says with a chuckle, and eyes the flimsy three-foot Christmas tree with amusement. "What a fucking waste of beer money."

Charlie watches multi-coloured lights twinkle through Duncan's fading image.

Maybe he would have some peace now.

Duncan is right, *what a waste of beer money*.

His head spins as he sits forward to reach for the vodka on the table—at least he didn't waste *all* his money.

Mack will be happy to see the tree, his dad dressed as Santa.

Charlie swallows spirits and goes to see his son.

He unlocks the six bolts.

His hands don't tremble like they did when he locked them. He pushes open the door; the smell hits him.

The fucking kid must have pissed the bed again. *Never mind, it's Christmas, he's only little.*

A chest of drawers, painted black, lies on its front, one of the drawers smashed against the cold, tiled floor. Black mould speckles the window surrounds as if the corruption from the town outside is creeping in at the seams.

Soggy wallpaper hangs in loose strips like ribbons of flayed flesh.

"What the fuck you done to your room, Mack?" Charlie says, shaking over his son's betrayal. The bed is a mess: little more than blankets strewn on the filthy floor. He thrusts a thumb into the crust of vomit on his chest. "I dressed as Father Christmas to surprise you, and this is what you do? Why, Son, why?"

Mack is hardly recognisable: his hair is different, he has grown, he wears different clothes than usual, he is in dire need of a bath.

For a moment, Charlie worries it's not even his son. *Why is my son so scared and dirty? Why is my son holding the front of a drawer like a baseball bat?*

Charlie frowns, but when he moves into the room, all is well, as it should be.

Posters on the wall, and toys, toys, toys.

Mack is back to his normal, cheeky little six year old self, the cute mess of blonde curls the same as Beth's when she'd been little. He has her eyes, too, and they beam up at him with childish glee as he sees his dad dressed as Father Christmas.

Mack holds something in his hand; Charlie can't make out what it is, a teddy bear or something.

He can't focus.

"What's that, Mackay boy? What you got for me, son?"

"I'm not your fucking son!" he says, and swings the teddy bear around for his old dad to give it a kiss .

3.

Charlie aspirates, sits up, and coughs gruel into his lap. His left eye is welded shut with something sticky, his head hurts so much it makes him retch when he touches it to inspect it for injuries.

His hand comes back red.

He is on the floor of his empty spare room and has no idea how he got there, or why he is dressed as Santa.

On his hands and knees, he goes into the lounge, slumps onto the sofa using the seat as a backrest, and looks lazily through the window.

The sky outside is a spectrum of orange, grey and navy blue, the closest it gets to complete darkness in the town centre.

Charlie isn't sure if it's early morning or night. He snorts through the back of his nose and fights the wave of hot nausea that comes as snot slides down the back of his throat like an oyster.

Coughs wrack his chest; he grabs hold of the Christmas tree; it topples over the coffee table and onto the floor.

"Now you see it," says Leon O'Hara, a vision with sparse hair, perpetually running nostrils; a lightbulb shaped head.

He waves a hand theatrically over the gap where the tree was, then claps his hands, splaying his fingers wide. "Now you don't!"

"Merry Christmas, Leon," Charlie says, smiling at his childhood friend. "Love you, mate."

Leon gives the smallest of smiles before taking a seat on the sofa, his back ramrod straight, hands on knees. "My name's Leon, and I love magic."

"Hocus pocus," Charlie says, and just like magic, he notices there is still half a bottle of vodka left.

Leon nods, passing his hands slowly in front of his face.

A blast of Mariah Carey singing one of her festive hits floats through into his fortress.

"Remember this one?" says Matt, lowering his hands, smoothing back wet hair over the bloody, caved-in section of his skull. He wipes his palms on the sofa. "She was the only woman I ever fancied."

None of the windows are open; the music has no right entering his flat.

"Fucking neighbours," Charlie slurs, and swigs from the bottle.

"Everybody needs good neighbours," Matt sings and walks over the fallen tree and decorations.

I don't want a lot for Christmas...

Charlie doesn't want a lot for Christmas, he doesn't even want *Christmas*, so why is there a fucking tree?

He kicks it across the room until it huddles in the corner, victimised and injured, the red baubles trailing behind it like blood. Charlie crushes each one into a sharp, glittery mess.

Why have I wasted money on a tree? There is nothing in the room that can answer his question, nothing out of the ordinary, just the normal garbage.

Then he spots the alien object on the coffee table, the lower half of a Christmas card, Santa's legs trampling through the snow.

He doesn't dare touch it, fears the familiar tiny handwriting inside.

Remembers what it says.

Merry Christmas, Charlie,
Maybe when you get yourself sorted; Mack will come round.
You'll be able to meet Angus.
Best wishes,
Beth, Adam, and Mack.

Is that why he bought the damn tree?

Is that why he dressed up as Father fucking Christmas?

Duncan chuckles from the darkness of the kitchen. "Your kid's twenty-four, you daft cunt, why the fuck would he want to see Santa?"

Charlie closes the sliding hatch between lounge and kitchen.

He is never festive.

Even when Mack was growing up, he was always a miserable bastard at Christmas.

They called him The Grinch, Beth and Mack, lovingly, jokingly at first. Maybe his heart was two sizes too small, too.

The last Christmas he remembers enjoying was when he was a kid.

This time of the year is suffocating. You can choke to death on the false happiness and goodwill.

Everybody left him in December.

Mum.

Dad.

Michael's motorcycle accident was during that lull between Boxing Day and New Year.

Even poor, sweet Leon; brain haemorrhage.

For Charlie, December is about taking, not receiving. Winter claimed more than its fair share of his family and friends.

The ghosts always show up to pay their respects at Christmas, whether you welcome them or not.

There's just one thing I need…

"Fucking Mariah Carey again, bastards must have it on repeat." Duncan stares down at him in his semi-comatose state.

"Fuck off!" Charlie barely whispers as he mashes the neck of the vodka bottle between his gums.

He needs to drink himself into a coma to get rid of the presence underneath his Christmas tree.

Somewhere in his jumble of a brain, he knows his visitations are mutated growths on some rotten morsel buried in his psyche. Post traumatic stress or something, someone told him once, he forgets where, when and who.

Charlie pulls the throw off the sofa and wraps it around himself, hugging the vodka bottle like a baby, vaguely wondering about the mess in the spare bedroom.

He dozes.

4.

When he wakes, the room is black and freezing. The throw is gone. The tip of his nose is numb with the cold, as is every other exposed patch of skin. The balcony door is open wide. Something flaps in the darkness.

From somewhere else, Mariah Carey continues.

The last few inches of vodka slosh in the bottle. He knocks it back and closes the door. It makes little difference but he draws the one remaining curtain against the purple night and the flashing blue lights.

Liquorice, black and thick like chunks of leather, engulfs him.

He is still there.

Charlie ignores the apparition and curses his increasing tolerance for spirits.

All kinds.

Sweet, unconscious oblivion is the only way to deal with Duncan. He is always in the room, but now he is stronger than ever. Charlie feels him, hears the whine of his congested lungs.

He forces himself forwards, away from the presence, unable to resist confrontation anymore. "No, you're not real! You're in my head." The doctors said it was possible to talk yourself out of these episodes.

Duncan laughs in his face and Charlie pisses himself.

He tries to regulate his breathing. *Yoga breathing, in, one, two, three, hold, out, two, and*—projectile vomit.

"Come, come with me, down Diamond Drive," Duncan, more solid than ever before, starts to croon.

Charlie stands in his wet pyjama bottoms as Duncan sings the lyrics of the children's programme that has haunted him for a lifetime.

"No!" he screams; his eyes blur with tears and he swings the vodka bottle by the neck. The bottle arcs through the freezing air and strikes the chimney breast, showering his hand with shards of glass.

Duncan laughs and begins whistling the theme tune he was singing. He spins in the centre of the room, arms out like the comedian at the start of the old children's programme. His non-corporeal body fades out into the coffee table.

"You're not there!" Charlie yells, and swings the broken bottle through Duncan's body. "You're not there!"

Tears flow as he says it again; this time, it's more of a plea. "You're not there!"

"Oh, but I am, Jacob," Duncan says, and Charlie feels cold fingers encircle his wrist. Charlie opens his eyes, shocked by the tangible contact, and sees Duncan half-illuminated by the blue lights that come through the window.

The moonlight picks out the warped craters of his burnt skin, and the hollow where his left eye once was is deep, dark, edged with a crescent of white bone. Charlie screams at the apparition, wrenches his hand from its grasp, the jagged bottom of the broken vodka bottle rakes across his exposed throat.

He whimpers at the pain, at the gash in his neck. Duncan laughs as arterial blood from Charlie's neck decorates the wall. Charlie staggers forwards, drops the bottle, clutches the throw to the ragged wound.

He falls onto the settee, reaches towards his phone.

Leon O'Hara smiles sadly, "Now you see him, now you don't."

"No," Charlie gurgles. The battery icon flashes empty; he drops the phone, too weak to move.

Duncan hangs over him.

Charlie can't keep his hand against the gash in his throat; his arm flops down, the throw, sodden with blood, gathers in his wet lap.

"Come, come with me down Diamond Drive," sings Duncan, one burnt hand held out waiting whilst Charlie dies.

Charlie sees the last intact Christmas bauble on the massacred tree through Duncan's transparent chest — it's like a heart.

Blackness creeps in around the seams of the room, just like the mould in the spare room where he kept the boy.

Like Duncan, he too is fading.

Charlie welcomes the sweet oblivion like a forgotten friend, for he is sure that nobody — not even Duncan — can follow him where he's going.

Inside

Your Frightful Spirit Stayed

1.

The dream always begins the same way.

Fists of khaki anorak.

A gaunt, red-cheeked youth with a ruby clown smirk of blood above his crooked mouth.

It turns from a bemused sneer to a shocked 'O' in the millisecond that he realises Charlie's let go of his coat, he's flying through the air. Charlie sees the lad's white fingers reach out to grab hold of the wall, bannister, anything, as he goes back into the stairwell.

At the foot of the stairs: a security guard, late fifties, dark glasses, obviously-dyed black moustache and hair. Charlie recognises him from the shopping centre. He looks like Andy Kauffman's alter-ego, Tony Clifton.

The shoplifter smashes into the sloped ceiling above the stairs. His head snaps forward along with his body as he drops to the metal-edged steps. He lands hard, rolls backwards, goes head-over-heels three times, his head and neck buffering, whipping at unnatural angles with each rotation. He comes to a stop upside-down at the security guard's feet, body lying awkwardly on the steps, head between polished boots.

Charlie rushes down the stairs but can already see death in the boy's eyes. He's seen it before. Tony Clifton removes his glasses, looks up at Charlie as if he's about to have a stroke, and the spectacles in his hand melt into a wooden gavel, his black jacket puffs out bat-wings into Judge Griffin's ceremonial robes.

Clifton's face stays the same, his accusatory stare the only thing that remains solid as everything else bleeds into the rich mahogany of the courtroom. Legal suits, pinched faces, bright overhead lights, a silence broken only by breath.

Clifton is now Judge Griffin; the words that come out of his mouth are nonsensical, forgotten, misheard and incomprehensible to Charlie as he stands awaiting his sentence.

The jurors are all people he knows.

They all stand with their index fingers pointing at him as though they're about to cry 'witch.'

Leon O'Hara is in the front row; twin, translucent slug trails glisten from nostril to lip. In one of his flattened palms is a rotary dial telephone, shiny red. He gazes at it in pure wonder, big, wet, happy tears in his eyes. Beside him, Shane, exactly how Charlie remembers him on television, older and thinner than when they were kids, bald and gaunt with hooded eyes that seem capable of holding more than just the one secret.

Johnny, Shane's cohort, is how Charlie had seen him last: short and rodenty with a scruff of hair that was a nondescript colour, somewhere strange between blonde and black. Matt is next to Leon, handsome, well-groomed, muscular, but with half his head caved in and dripping. A figure wearing a motorcycle helmet and leathers run ragged by the road stands behind his friends. Michael's a zombie, living dead roadkill. Further along is a hospital bed stood vertical with a shrivelled, yellow corpse-thing that used to be his father. It's as weak and brittle as a day-old chick but manages to raise a finger. Charlie's brother is propped up by his dear old mum who just cries and cries and cries and cries between her tarmac-infused eldest and cancer-kissed husband.

Another juror is Michelle, that lovely girl he'd got too close to at work; the *bit of fun* as she had called it happened more than once, and he wasn't able to let it go as easily as she did. Beth is next; she eyes Michelle with hypocritical, jealous rage, Charlie still feels the bitterness of her infidelity even in his dream, even after all these years.

Mack, his beautiful boy, is familiar, but a stranger beside his mother. This is a future image of him, his vista never stays still, he rapidly blurs through puberty into a man before his eyes, becoming taller, broader, hairier, all the things Charlie is going to miss.

"You're going down, ain't you?"

Judge Griffin lifts his wig to reveal a burnt, bald scalp and half-distinguished facial features. The man with two faces, Duncan will be the one to pass judgment on him.

"You're going down, —" he says another name other than Charlie and it takes Charlie far too long to remember it still means him. More words come out of Duncan but Charlie now spots Two-Bags the shoplifter by his feet, bloody nose, neck bent the wrong way, dead, but not letting a minor technicality like death stop him from cackling up at his murderer and hissing abuse.

All speak at once, their words and phrases varying in length and tone, to the backing track of a motorcycle crash. Together, they make a strange and hateful choir.

"Murderer!"

"You're going down!"

"Now you see him, now you don't!"

"It was only a bit of fun, Charlie, we were both drunk."

"Nonce."

"Dad."

"I'm dying, son."

"Why couldn't you just talk to me?"

And presiding over it all is Duncan. The gavel, as if by a magical zap from master magician Leon O'Hara, has exploded into a rainbow umbrella and it's now raining on the courtroom as he dances and sings. *"Come, come with me down Diamond Drive."* And the rain is red, red, red and the people all begin to sing the same words now, the same word.

Murderer

Murderer

Murderer

Murderer

Murderer

Murderer

2.

Charlie wakes up in a panic. For a moment, he thinks he's back there with Duncan, that his whole fucking life is a sickening, lucid dream, and that the worst is yet to come—again. It's not, though, for although he hates where he is nearly as much as where he was, there are at least more rules here, at least an ounce of safety.

His feverish panting slows and the fingertips of one hand brush the metal base of Ogilvy's bunk—only lightly, though.

He doesn't want to wake that brutish man and have seven shades of shit beaten out of him like the week before, just for crying out in his sleep.

Charlie listens to Ogilvy's snores: peaceful, no troubled sleep for those without conscience.

The same four walls.
The same iron door.
The same barred window and the same pan to shit in.

Charlie checks once again, over his shoulder, that Ogilvy is sound as a house before emptying his bladder.

His clothes have gotten too big again.

He notices as he pulls the elasticated waistband up that he has to fold and pleat the material more before tucking it in on itself. Today he will get a smaller pair of trousers, or forget again.

Charlie is always by the cell door when the wardens unlock it, ready to head to a place where there are more people.

Safety in numbers.

He nods at Warden Carter, a man half his age and twice his size, hairless and built like a rhino. Warden Carter nods back, lets him by before growling for Ogilvy to shift his arse.

The mess hall is a murmur of yawns, grunts and catarrh-laced coughs.

Charlie never ate breakfast before jail and nothing much has changed in the five years he's been inside.

The anxiety is now permanent; he imagines his innards clenched in a giant's fist.

As he takes toast and butter he notices blood spots on his sleeves from the scratching he does at night.

Charlie takes his food and a lukewarm mug of coffee to a table; sits alone.

The chair beside him scrapes back and somebody sits silently.

They bring with them the familiar pungency: body odour, cigarettes, and liquorice.

As Charlie reaches for the plastic butter knife, a leathered claw clamps around his wrist. He's not safe from Duncan, even in here.

Trying to free his hand is pointless, Duncan is always too strong. He pushes Charlie's hand down, snapping the plastic knife blade at an angle, turning it into a lengthy point. Charlie struggles as Duncan forces his hand upwards, the sharp shard on a slow path towards his face.

"No," Charlie cries at long last, inmates close enough to hear and to casually look up between mouthfuls.

One of the wardens catches on to what's happening and shouts his name, but before he can cross the mess hall, Duncan has stabbed that plastic pick into Charlie's cheek.

Charlie feels it enter his mouth, grate against a tooth, dig into the side of his tongue. Duncan pulls on his wrist, trying to get a second attack in. Charlie goes to move, but the warden jumps on him, pinning him down. The warden in charge stomps across the canteen. "Get him up to the infirmary, stick him back on suicide watch. Daft bastard."

Duncan loves it when Charlie is on suicide watch, where they take everything away that he can think of using to hurt himself. They, the wardens, are supposed to keep an eye on him, check on him every fifteen minutes, but often they forget—for hours and hours on end.

Charlie doesn't mind the solitude, but he hates the company. You're never truly alone with a friend like Duncan.

As soon as they've patched him up, wrapped him in cotton wool, he's thrown in a cell where the walls don't feel real.

"Ah," Duncan says, his voice a whisper on the nape of his neck, "just like old times."

It's what he always says once they are finally left alone together after the doctors and nurses have finished faffing and the shrink has had a half-arsed word about the probability of prescription changes.

Just like old times.

Duncan spits his vengeful hate at him; nobody else hears it.

He hurts Charlie; nobody sees it.

He touches Charlie with scarred hands, rough as sandpaper, cold as frost.

When he tells the shrinks about his visitations, they tell him he does these things to himself, can even show him CCTV footage. It reminds him of the Brad Pitt film that came out just before he got done for murder, the one where he plays an imaginary friend. Duncan's nowhere near as good-looking.

The doctors change his medication and sometimes Duncan vanishes for a while but when he comes back he always returns more livid than ever, as though the place where he's been imprisoned has been medieval in its torture.

His attacks take on a new severity. Charlie quickly learns that it's easier to say nothing, hide the tablets, give Duncan free rein.

Things reach an aching kind of stability, then.

3.

Charlie's never intentionally tried to kill himself. He doesn't have the bottle. That's why he thinks Duncan is real, not a part of him.

He longs for peace, an end to it all, but the thing he wants an end to is his existence, not his life.

He wants a new start, a new existence, a new body, new past, new present, new future. Charlie doesn't want to be Charlie anymore.

He tries to focus on when he gets out [he won't be here forever] and the things he thinks he will do.

In his daydreams, he imagines getting back with Beth, but knows that he lacks imagination—and only wants that because it's familiar. *She's* familiar, like an old coat.

He dreams of seeing his son, Mack, meeting Mack's son, but hasn't heard from either Mack or Beth since his conviction a decade earlier.

If it wasn't for his mum, he wouldn't have known he was a grandfather.

He tells himself that once he's out, even though he'll be an old man, he can start again, and for a few hours he will feel happy—amongst images of a quaint little flat near a pub and a park. There would be things he would be, things he could do to build himself a life again.

But they wouldn't last. They would never last.

Duncan always infiltrates his head, blackening the brightest of dreams.

A dream of something real that was described but never seen.

Not by Charlie's eyes, anyway.

A yellow-walled hospital ward.

A curtained bed.

A hunched, weeping shadow.

Through the blue patterned material is a woman who has seen too much loss in her life; the only thing that holds her to the soil is the one decent thing either of her sons did: her grandson, Mack. She speaks in hushed tones to the husk of a man beneath the blankets on the bed. He isn't expected to last the night but still wants to hear about his beloved grandson.

"Mackay's doing well at school. He did come the other night, but you were asleep. It's a pain in the arse on the train but he'd be up here every night if we let him." She holds the weak hand in hers. "He's the dead spit of his dad."

Charlie spots disappointment in her eyes, more sorrow. She acts like she's lost two sons, both he and Michael.

Charlie's dad whispers something behind the mask as his mum leans closer to catch what he's saying, desperate to cling on, for soon these will be his last words.

"I know it's not his fault," she says mournfully, "but how was it your fault?"

Charlie's dad manages to say something else before coughing takes control. He looks sure to shatter.

"Don't talk daft. Every dad shows their mates pictures of their kids." His mum has tears in her eyes and so does his dad.

Charlie knows what he means; his father knew Duncan once upon a time. A casual drinking buddy.

His dad dies without another word and with a heart full of guilt.

Work

Your Frightful Spirit Stayed

1.

It's too hot but he sips it anyway.

Sweet black tea is the only thing he can stomach at such an early hour.

Charlie doesn't have a problem with early starts but his body hates them.

His stomach bubbles and churns with anxiety even though he knows there is no reason for it. He leans against the kitchen worktop; he never sits down first thing in the morning for fear of falling back to sleep.

Charlie is not a morning person.

"Alright, Dad?" Mack says, shuffling groggily into the kitchen in just his school trousers.

Charlie grunts and yawns. He watches his boy go about his morning routine.

Even though Mack is eleven, he has the physique of someone older.

Kids seem bigger these days. Charlie was nowhere near as tall as Mack when he was his age.

His son stretches his arms up towards the ceiling.

He even has defined muscles, for Christ's sake.

Filling the four-slice toaster with bread, he slams the racks down and reaches up for a juice glass. Mack's eyes have slight dark circles beneath them and as Charlie automatically hands him the juice carton, his father speaks for the first time that day.

"How late were you awake 'til?"

Mack shrugs. "Dunno, think it was about one. Had to watch the last episode of AHS, man, but there was an extra episode to the second season, not like the first."

Charlie shakes his head; he doesn't know how his son can stay awake until the early hours of the morning and still be functional in time for school. Also, he never understands how he can go to sleep after watching such ludicrously horrifying films and programmes.

There is no point in restricting what he watches when Beth lets him watch whatever he likes. Charlie has never understood the fascination of the genre, maybe if Beth and his son had faced true horrors or real monsters first-hand, they would have a different outlook.

A wave of cold passes over him and he thinks of another horror fan.

His mother.

He has promised he will take Mack to the hospital to visit his father later, something he has put off for the last week or so.

Now, what his dad is going through is real horror.

Knowing that no matter how healthy a life he tried to live, it was all for nothing.

Kidney failure for a fucking retirement present. Hours on dialysis, the wonderful plans for his autumn years ruined.

A lifetime of working hard to spend the last years of his life with the woman he loved, tainted.

All for nothing. Glorious country hikes now turned into illness and inactivity.

Charlie watches as his son walks across the kitchen brushing toast crumbs off his face and chest.

As though reading his father's mind, Mack pivots around and tugs at his work shirt sleeve. "So, are we going to see Grandad tonight?"

Charlie stacks his cup into an already full sink and rubs a hand over the stubble he's forgotten to shave.

He considers the ninety-minute drive after working an eight-hour day.

If he doesn't take him, and the worst happens, it will be another layer of guilt to line the one already coating the insides of his stomach. Not only that, he will never hear the end of it from Beth.

"Okay, but you've got to remember he's not going to be like how you remembered him last year. The meds, the radiotherapy, takes a lot out of him."

"I know, Dad." Mack nods sincerely.

"Alright, as long as you're prepared."

Charlie watches his son pale a little as he pierces the juice carton with a straw and wonders who the kid was putting on a brave face for.

Your Frightful Spirit Stayed

2.

The pangs begin as he says goodbye to Mack and pulls away from the school. It is the first time he has experienced them during the week in a long time — well, two years, at least.

After his marriage ended, drink became a regular crutch that he leant on almost every single weekend, but never to the extent that it affected his work. When he began to get cravings for alcohol during the week, when the journey from Monday to Friday seemed impossible to bear without extra help, he cut it out.

His life has been a vicious cycle of trying to mask things with different disguises.

He can feel it. The swelling inside him that has been there for decades is sick of being mollycoddled with prescription drugs and is ready to be born again. A black sun that has waited patiently for another chance to shine, and fill his two-year pre-dawn with its black sunrise.

Charlie tries to concentrate on the road, but once he feels the beginnings of that suffocation, the tell-tale pressure on his shoulders (not a physical one, just yet), he finds it difficult to ignore.

The sound of car horns clears the fog. They are for him.

A green light hangs above.

As he starts the car, it changes to amber so he lets it stall again.

More irritation, inside and out.

How long has he been sitting here?

Fuck's sake, pull yourself together.

He unwinds the window, checks his watch, thanks God he is still making good time.

Concentrate.

He focuses on the road ahead, his hands on the steering wheel.

He tries not to notice the silvery, self-harm scar that's just been exposed by his rising sleeve.

Yoga breathing, in through the nose, hold, one, two, three, out through the mouth. Slowly.

You did that with a kitchen knife when Beth told you she was leaving you after you found her with Adam.

Charlie takes the road into town, trying to ignore his self-hatred, but finds it hard to shut his mind.

You did it whilst Mackay was in the house. You sad, pathetic, prat. Did you think she would change her mind, stay?

"Fuck off!" Charlie hisses and pulls into the multi-storey car park.

He parks in the nearest spot, lurches across the passenger seat to grab the steering wheel lock from the footwell.

A faint whiff of liquorice stops him as he sits back up; he feels instantly sick.

"No, no, no." He does not have time for this shit, he has work.

He fastens the wheel lock, grabs his bag, and leaves the car as quickly as he can.

Charlie dodges commuters and heads towards his shop.

His job is one of the few things in his life that doesn't use up too much of his tolerance levels, even though he hates it. Ninety per cent of the time it is ideal, a doss, but not easy enough for his mind to be left unoccupied for hours on end.

Some days fall into the other ten percentile.

His love for retail has soured over the years he has devoted to it, but overall, it's bearable, and he knows he has never had the mental capacity for anything more demanding.

A puddle of something that is either regurgitated curry or diarrhoea runs down the metal shutters and collects in a heap on the tiled floor at the entrance. It clogs in the shutters' keyhole.

He opens the shutters and gets the undetermined substance on his knuckles.

He curses head office for the millionth time that they won't fork out on automatic shutters like all the other shops in the row. As he heaves the filthy metal up so he can gain entrance, he catches the eye of the manager of the shoe shop next door.

Charlie hates the smarmy prick. He is always pristinely turned-out, always in his shop well before him, with its glossy automatic roll shutters that slide up and down almost silently. All the window displays are immaculate; even litter doesn't seem to gather in his doorway.

He always acts as though they are in competition even though Charlie's shop is a branch of stationers.

Charlie grins a good morning through clenched teeth, opens the door with one hand, and slips into the cold shop.

"Ah, for fuck's sake." Charlie slams his palms against his face and switches the PC off. It isn't his day.

First, the shit on the doorstep he had to scrub off — no amount of washing could convince him his hands were clean enough, but when he checks the work emails he has received, he finds one from his knob of a regional manager who is making a surprise visit to talk to him about the recent spate of shoplifting.

In the regional manager's words, his store is the worst in the region; it isn't good enough.

The town is rife with shoplifting scumbags. Most of them he recognises by sight as they pace back and forth, the shoplifters' flightpath of the high street. Scruffy junkie bastards begging, scrounging in between nipping in and out of the stores, stealing on demand.

They are so familiar with one another, he and the regular shoplifters, that they know not to come into the shop if he is in there. He has caught them red handed many times.

Laminators, shredders, printers, and ink cartridges are the go-to items, expensive things they can sell cheap for a profit. It has reached the point where Charlie can't even have a break without something being stolen. Small shops like his never have enough staff. Head office gives them just enough manpower to scrape by but they rarely think about break times and sickness.

Gladys, a feeble mole rat of a woman, has been his assistant manager forever, shipped over from one of the nearby smaller town branches that closed, against his will. She is more of a hindrance than a help and he knows the petty criminals of the town love it when she is in charge for the day.

He hears her distinctive tread as she comes up the stairs, her heavy breaths of exertion as she walks through the small warehouse above the shop.

"Good morning."

"There's nothing good about it," Charlie moans, and smashes his forehead against his desk.

"I know what you've been up to. I know you better than you know yourself," Gladys snorts, rolling her eyes and gawping through the grimy glass of the warehouse window at the passers-by.

She is a barrage of clichés.

"And what, pray tell, have I been up to, Gladys?"

"You've been on the booze again. You're hungover. I can tell."

Charlie bites back the anger boiling inside. "I've not touched a drop for nearly two years, Gladys, although knowing that Wetherspoons is open right now, that it was payday yesterday, and Mark fucking Grant is coming today to talk about the shoplifting is certainly making me want to jump back off the wagon, I can tell you."

"Don't know what you're going to do about that," Gladys shrugs with the same indifference she applies to everything.

"We, Gladys, *we*."

"You're the manager," she says with a shrug, and moves next door to the staffroom.

Within seconds, he hears the kettle start to boil.

"Yeah, I'm the fucking manager," Charlie half-cries to himself.

3.

Charlie wishes Gladys would die in her sleep. He gets the phone call on his lunch break: his dad isn't expected to last the night. It's the second time they've said that, though, and Gladys, *that fucking bitch*, never answers her phone on her days off.

She's a cunt.

He stares out of the shop window, cursing every passing person to hell.

When he took Mack to see his dad the previous month, he looked perkier than he had for years.

Charlie wants to close the shop and drive the ninety minutes to see his father, but knows it will likely cost him his job.

"You sure you're alright, Charlie?" Michelle, the twenty-four-year-old part-timer says with genuine concern. "You ain't at it with the banter this afternoon."

They usually spend the last couple of quiet hours chatting with one another.

Although she is twenty years younger than him, they get on well. A little *too* well, if after-hours alcohol is involved.

He relives the hours spent on her sofa every time he's lonely, sometimes it saves his life, sometimes it almost ends it. He knows he hired her because she was attractive, appeared to have a brain and a sense of humour. That, and she reminded him of Beth when they first met — and there was a large part of him that never left his early twenties.

Even though he is closer to fifty than forty, he still feels he has missed out on life somewhere.

"Just not with it today, mate. To be honest with you, I can't wait to knock off." He manages to force a grin; he doesn't divulge anything about his private life to her anymore. He can't stand the pitiful looks, and if she hugged him he'd only want to fuck her, and they swore they weren't going to do that again.

It isn't worth the hassle.

The oppression that has been building up over the past couple of months finally got the better of him last week and he came off the wagon with a vengeance.

Upstairs in his coat pocket is a half-litre bottle of vodka. A glance at his watch tells him he has half an hour before the rush-hour customers come in on their way home from their offices, schools, and colleges.

"Just nipping to the toilet," Charlie tells Michelle as she tidies the till area.

He leaves the shop floor, flies up the stairs to retrieve the vodka bottle from his pocket. The liquid burn promises to take all his problems away if he just has one more swig.

Across the warehouse, the two-tone klaxon of the bell at the till goes off. He swears, stashes the bottle away, and bolts back down the stairs.

"No, put it back!" he hears Michelle shout; she sounds like Beth when they met, ballsy and full of life.

Charlie steps through the aisles to see what the commotion is.

Michelle stands in the shop doorway, blocking a hooded figure from leaving.

Charlie recognises him immediately.

It is one of the lifters he calls *Two-Bags* because of the crisscross of drawstring gym bags he always wears.

Something bulges beneath his dirty anorak; he sees the boy turn around and spot him. Rust-coloured hair spills out from under his hood. His scrawny red cheeks flush, he spins back around to Michelle and spits on her.

"You dirty little twat!" Michelle says, looking down at the glob of phlegm on the front of her fleece.

Charlie runs towards the front of the shop. Two-Bags growls at Michelle and shoves her into a stack of printer paper.

"You fucking little bastard!" Charlie is barely aware of what he is doing until he has the youth in a headlock and is dragging him back further into the shop.

"Here, have 'em!" Two-Bags chokes out and a peg full of printer cartridges falls out of his coat, the security tags still attached.

Usually, Charlie would let them go, then, it wasn't worth it once they'd handed the stuff back, but something snapped when he saw him assault Michelle.

Michelle is on her feet in a matter of seconds and looking towards her manager for orders. They aren't supposed to apprehend shoplifters.

"Get on the link to security in the centre." Charlie nods towards the phone behind the till at a list of numbers that have faded over time. "Tell them what he's done and that I'm holding him in the office."

Two-Bags dares to mock, "You're having a laugh, they won't do nothing, you daft prick."

"We'll see about that," Charlie sneers, and frogmarches him through the shop.

"They never do mate," Two-Bags says, willingly being led. "I get collared at least once a month."

Charlie pushes the shop floor door open and points towards the stairs. "And how many times have you assaulted a shop worker?"

The ginger boy pales, changes tactics. "Look, man, I can't help it. I've got to do it. I owe people money."

"Not my problem." Charlie doesn't want to hear his sob story, everybody has one. "Up the stairs."

Two-Bags stomps up the stairs ahead of him and begins sniffling. He turns, tears in his eyes, "Come on man, I'm only fifteen."

"I don't care! You and your mates are always nicking from me and I've had enough, do you hear? You don't give a shit about the kind of trouble I get into so why should I care about what trouble *you* get into?"

"You just don't get it," Two-Bags says, scoping out the warehouse. "I steal cuz I need to."

"Whatever," Charlie says, blocking the only exit, the stairs, keeping one eye on the shoplifter and the other on the door below as he eagerly awaits the cavalry.

The security in the shopping centre will only take five minutes, max.

"You could get into trouble, too," Two-Bags says, smiling when he sees Charlie's face blanch with worry. "Trapping a minor."

"Don't talk such bollocks, you stole from my shop. They probably know you by name. The police and all." Charlie fakes amusement at the boy's words but it is a paper-thin facade and he knows the kid can see through it.

"Yeah," Two-Bags swaggers with confidence once he realises he has found a way to get under Charlie's skin. "I'm only fifteen, man, and there's you, a fat, single, old man."

Charlie turns his back on him and tries his best to focus on the door and the bottom of the stairs, willing the shopping centre security to show up. He won't allow the little prick to wind him up, it's what people like him want, to drag you down to their level. He'll make sure the dick stays where he is until the guards come.

He closes his eyes and wonders what is taking them so long. The pungent tang of liquorice surrounds him and it is so familiar that he isn't at all surprised by its presence. His anxiety levels have reached critical levels and he knows as soon as the guards have taken the piece of shit away, he will finish the rest of the vodka in his coat pocket.

Fuck the kid and fuck this job.

He opens his eyes and sees misty vapours creeping in at the sides of his vision.

He flinches and instantly thinks this is another one of his full-on visitations, right here in front of the shoplifter. The signs have been happening again the last few weeks, they always come with the stress, the audible and olfactory hallucinations; the alcohol only exacerbates them.

"Chill man, it's only a vape pen."

Charlie jolts at the sound of Two-Bags' voice. The kid sits against a pile of boxed stock, puffing aniseed-flavoured smog into the warehouse.

He laughs at Charlie's frightened pose, a leering malevolence twisting his face. "Let me go or I'll tell the coppers you touched me. Tried it on, like. You look like a fucking nonce."

The monster that lives deep within Charlie's chest and stomach rushes up into his head, his arms, and he roars at the kid.

There is no sensation as Charlie's fist connects with Two-Bags' cheek, no sound as his foot slams into the kid's ribcage.

He hears him shout the word 'paedo', though, as the lad lies on the floor laughing with a nose full of blood.

Rage is all-consuming, rage is God, as Charlie heaves the boy up by the front of his anorak and hurls him towards the steep stairs.

Return to Goswell's Wood

1.

Beth was so fucking cute when Charlie met her, all pale-skinned and pink-lipped. Every aspect of her was the pinnacle of his sexual desires.

He watches her now from the corner of his eye as she sits on the sofa, still in her dressing gown at half-past two in the afternoon.

Even the sight of her in pyjamas used to turn him on. Jesus, *everything* about her used to turn him on.

Then.

It isn't even the weight she has put on, it's nothing physical, he isn't that shallow, she is still the beautiful girl he fell in love with — but somehow the years have diluted that, watered down the magic into something ordinary.

He is used to her, perhaps even bored.

Mack is at nursery, they have an hour before they have to get him and they are sitting at opposite sides of the room, she picking her nose and texting whilst watching daytime soaps, and he staring at Instagram models ten years younger than her.

A decade ago, their synchronised days off would have been fun-filled, with sex marathons, day trips, and talking.

They did stuff.

Now they barely say a word to each other unless the kid is there.

"Texting your boyfriend, are you?"

Almost every remark he makes is laced with poison he will never admit to. It's never meant to be taken seriously; he is only ever joking, even though there is never any hint of humour.

Beth rolls her eyes. "Well, he's saying more than you are."

Charlie scowls at her, he knows she has refrained from speaking her usual lines of reassurance on purpose — to antagonise him.

He refuses to rise to it, preferring to fester.

With a sigh, he forces himself to change his attitude and diffuses the situation before it gets any worse. "Work's been fucking shit. The people of this town are fucking idiots."

"Have you got anywhere with those jobs you were looking at online?" she says, not taking her eyes from the TV and phone.

"No, they're all shit." He can't tell her that after spending five minutes while she was on night shift looking at better jobs than his, he'd spent three hours watching porn, looking at better women than his.

His brother's forewarning a decade before echoes in his mind daily, amidst the other voices.

Don't run away with the first bird who opens her legs for you.

And he worries over Michael's words like an aching tooth, constantly poking to check they still hurt. That's exactly what he did, smitten or not, and for some reason, this has grown into bitter resentment at the once-upon-a-time girl of his dreams. As though it's all her fault.

Beth sighs and throws her phone on the settee. "Are you going to this reunion thing?"

Charlie thinks about the school reunion. "It's fucking weird."

"Why is it weird?"

"No one has reunions for primary schools."

"So what? This is a special thing, though, innit?"

Charlie nods and thinks about the letter that his mum passed onto him.

Mrs Gough, *old Gough-Bags herself*, his teacher in the last, well, *only* full year at primary school back in the village, wanted to invite as many of the leavers that were in his, and her, last year there, to her eightieth birthday party. He thought she was old, then.

He understands the sentiment, but the idea of an evening back in the village does not appeal.

"You might be able to hook up with some old mates," Beth says, picking her phone back up. He sees her eyes flick across a message and a huge grin blossoms.

It's been ages since he made her smile like that.

"You might bump into an old flame." There's a hint of his maliciousness in her tone and he doesn't like it at all, but he knows that to comment on it will make him a grade-A hypocrite.

"I'll think about it."

Your Frightful Spirit Stayed

2.

Charlie ends up leaving after all, even though he has no intention of going to the reunion until the moment he storms off to the train station.

The weather reflects his mood, dark and portentous.

Betrayal burns in his heart but it's swamped with guilt and self-loathing at how stupid he's been with his wife and best friend.

Adam.

Adam is his best friend.

Charlie never thought he would have a friendship that came anywhere close to the bond he had with his school friends as a teenager — until Adam came along. It's probably the best friendship he's ever had.

They met when Adam was going through a messy divorce, and, according to Adam, Charlie helped him get over it. It was rare for Charlie to warm to another man, he rarely shared the same interests with anyone, but they were alike, and so began a saga about two sad, fat ginger bastards.

Charlie was always happy to have Adam around, especially after Mack was born and they didn't go out as much.

When Adam's about, nobody has to be serious.

When Adam's about, there is always booze.

Beth almost always goes to bed with Mack and leaves them to it. Sometimes she doesn't mind, but when it's every Friday and Saturday night she begins to make subtle protests.

Charlie reminds her of how lonely Adam is after his wife broke his heart.

After his mother died the same year. Lathers on the guilt like thick buttercream.

Beth sighs and goes to bed.

But it's always laughter with Charlie and Adam. Laughter, music, nothing ever serious, but when Adam's younger sister is diagnosed with leukaemia, Charlie is useless. Adam talks more to Beth. She listens, understands, cares.

Charlie cares, too, but he never knows the right things to say. When people's moods are low, it reminds him of the bad things in his life. Charlie's susceptible to other people and their personalities, temperamental shifts, and during Adam's low periods, he develops his own. He feels like an attention-seeking arsehole for constantly mulling over something that affected him so long ago.

Charlie withdraws into self-pity and self-harm. He's learnt more subtle ways of smothering the hurt; the drink helps but also amplifies, scarring just raises questions, but gluttony, gluttony is great.

He stuffs himself with whatever carbohydrate or fat-laden treats he can find, as much as he can, and it freezes everything for the moment.

Adam's sister has taken a turn for the worse, she is not responding to her latest treatment. There's more to it, something medical that goes way, way over Charlie's head, and his friend has turned up in a state, wanting to speak to Beth.

The text messages aren't enough anymore, Adam's her friend more than his now, and the thought alone makes an insecure child of Charlie.

He stares out of the train window, checking his phone for text messages, but knows his phone hasn't gone off.
She never texts him anymore.

Unwelcome nostalgia smacks him in the face as he steps off the train at Manningtree. The stark wind is as unchangeable as the open grey expanse of the Victorian station. It's the coldest place on earth, one of the most depressing, too, for Charlie.
He pulls his coat around him and walks up the platform.
The headline board outside the paper shop says, 'FIVE YEARS ON: COLBERT STILL MISSING.' Charlie thinks, *well that's another one who won't be at Gough-Bag's little reunion,* and a pang of hurt stings as he realises Shane was the one he'd have liked to have met up with the most.
Out of his old friends, Shane was probably the only one on the same wavelength as him.
He gets a taxi to the Bull.

There's been a lot of modernization to the village since he came a few years back: new shops, new houses. As the taxi pulls up to the pub, they pass a shuttered bookshop and Charlie laughs. The village never did like its culture.

3.

The Bull has had a refit; it's quaintly lit but there's the wet-dog smell of damp coats.

He walks in and spots them instantly. They don't see him; he snaps his face towards the bar to hide his expression of shock.

Oh, Jesus fucking Christ, I can't do this, he thinks, as a lanky barman smiles at him.

"Pint of Guinness, please," he says, immediately regretting his choice as he realises how long the fucking thing takes to pour.

They sit on the other side of the pub. It's quite open plan, busy, but Charlie never forgets a face, although he often wishes he could. His heart breaks at the split-second glimpse he's had, and knows, whether he wants it or not, it's already imprinted in his mind.

Leon.

Leon has aged so, so fucking much.

He sits next to his mum, who still looks like she did back when they were kids, aside from a few grey hairs, but Leon resembles a tiny, shrunken imp.

Charlie and he are the same age, yet decrepitude has swamped him, he is now Middle Earth's Golem, dressed by Marks and Spencer.

Leon's little lightbulb-shaped head is now virtually bald, a few wispy strands are tucked down beside his ears, his face the same aside from signs of rapid age. He stares at his lap; elsewhere, hands that resemble dehydrated starfish rest on beige-trousered knees whilst his mum talks to an elderly woman dressed like the Queen, with a frilled, fancy hat balanced upon a coiffured blue rinse.

The one and only Gough-Bag.

Charlie can't remember who originally coined that nickname but he supposed it was a take on that horrid fat witch who pestered Rod Hull and Emu, *Grotbags*.

They were nothing alike, the TV witch and his old teacher, the name just seemed to fit.

"Fucking hell, looks like you discovered the finer things in life!"

Charlie turns; there's an athletic man in a white t-shirt and jeans, grinning at him.

His clothes are tight-fitting and show off a physique that has spent a large majority of its existence in gyms or playing sports. He still has the same unnaturally fair hair, as if he has Scandinavian ancestry.

Almost automatically—years of faking politeness at work have helped—Charlie reaches out his hand. "Matt!"

Matt frowns at his hand, says, "fuck that shit," and throws his arms around him in a strong bear hug.

After a few seconds, the embrace stops, Charlie quickly pays for his Guinness, Matt smiles at him. "Didn't think anyone would turn up in this weather. It's really good to see you again. We should never have lost touch."

It's nice to hear him say that; Charlie thinks the sentiment is genuine. "Are you living back this way, or?"

"No, no, I'm based in Manchester and Birmingham nowadays, mate, but I've got a hotel booked.

"Eh, there's a spare bed if you fancy catching up properly tonight?" He pauses, and when Charlie refrains from accepting or declining his offer, continues. "I just hoped to see some familiar faces, you know, but as yet, you're the only person I've recognised."

Charlie sips at his Guinness, says the inevitable, "Leon's here."

Matt's face lights up as he scans the busy pub. "He is? Oh, man, I loved that crazy little dude. Where is he?"

"Other side of the pub; I was just plucking up the courage to go over there. To be honest with you, I was going to down this and clear off once I saw how much he had aged." Charlie is surprised at himself, at how easy it is to talk to his old friend.

Matt has procured a fashionable Mexican bottled lager, as if from thin air.

Magic, just like Leon.

"Ain't going to be anyone else from our gang here."

"I know," Charlie says sadly, "that's why I was plucking up the courage to go over. I think I owe it to the little guy to see how he is."

"We both do, mate," Matt says, his eyes misted, "we should never have lost touch."

Charlie takes a larger gulp of Guinness to smother the emotions. "I think we were all shit-scared, and with what happened with Shane and Johnny after."

Matt nods solemnly and points a finger to the regal Mrs Gough. "If only she had wanted this do a few years earlier, maybe there would have been four of us."

"I doubt it," Charlie scoffs, "not with what I saw about the mighty Shane Colbert on the news. I think he only came back because his mum died."

"And then he went missing," Matt says, casually looking around for the barman. "What do you reckon happened there, then?"

Charlie hasn't thought about Shane's recent disappearance, but remembers how much of an outcast the villagers made him as a teenager after Johnny and his other friends went missing, how the small-minded folk around here never seemed to let things go.

"It wouldn't surprise me if someone still had a vendetta and he's buried out in someone's field somewhere." The words come out without him having any control, it's almost as if he can see them freezing in the air.

A look passes between them, one which tells them the shared nightmare of their past was more than just a figment of their imaginations.

Without a word, Matt orders them both another drink.

4.

The drinks come; they wind through the busy drinkers to the table on the far side of the pub.

It's Mrs O'Hara who looks at them first; even though her expression is polite, there is no hint of recognition. Mrs Gough slants her chin upwards towards them, her eyes glow with canny recollection. "Matthew Chappell and Charlie Lawrence." She says it with clear certainty and Charlie can't help but be impressed.

"Have we not changed that much, Miss?" Matt says with a chuckle.

"One gets used to watching people grow up when one reaches eighty." Mrs Gough sounds and looks exactly how he remembers.

Charlie notices Leon's head rise slightly towards him and is horrified to see milky cataracts on each of his eyes. A smile, *that same smile*, cracks Leon's face and Charlie's heart as he sees his old friend has hardly any teeth left. "Charlie?"

"Yeah, mate, it's good to see you." Charlie and Matt pull up a pair of chairs to the table.

Mrs O'Hara apologises for not recognising them, and after Charlie passes a couple of pleasantries on how neither lady has aged at all, Mrs O'Hara leans forward over the still-ecstatic Leon and says, "Charlie, can you pull your chair closer? Leon can't see so well these days. He's on a waiting list to have cataracts removed."

"Charlie!" Leon exclaims excitedly and Charlie moves his chair closer.

Leon sits forward and squints at Charlie and Matt in turn. "You got old."

Everyone at the table laughs simultaneously.

"Charlie!" Leon says, jerks back in his seat, and thrusts a hand into the pocket of a coat hanging on the back of his chair. He retrieves a small mint tin and makes a pretty good show at hiding it in his palm.

He lifts his hand beside Charlie's right ear and produces the tin seemingly out of thin air as he whispers, "Magic ear."

Charlie's laughter is genuine, it's the first time he's laughed like that for years.

It feels good.

"You've not lost your magic touch," Matt says, clapping, whistling.

"Oh, he's still obsessed, just like he ever was," Mrs O'Hara says, and pats her son on the arm. "Leon, why don't you show the boys what's inside the tin?"

For some reason, the Guinness in Charlie's belly bubbles uneasily.

This isn't Leon's tin, it's Pandora's fucking box, I just know it.

As Leon fumbles awkwardly, Charlie can't take his eyes from the little tin.

He can't breathe.

Palpitations flutter, there's a faint whiff: liquorice and the tang of sweat.

Some of the paint has worn away in places, he hasn't seen one of these tins since he used to go shopping with his mother.

Bloody Marks and Spencer.

Leon opens the hinged lid. Inside is a toffee penny wrapped in foil and gold-coloured cellophane, and something that looks like a pickled walnut.

The tension inside Charlie releases; the sound he makes is a missing link between anguish and joy. "No way!"

Mrs O'Hara proves something of a magician herself as she pulls a tissue from out of nowhere and dabs at her eyes.

Mrs Gough is rendered speechless by this secretive communion between Mrs O'Hara, Leon and Matt.

"Well, Charlie," Mrs O'Hara loses the tissue with another flourish, "are you going to tell them why you're so gobsmacked?"

Charlie takes a moment and a sip of his drink to wet his throat, "My first day at Brooklands..."

Leon butts in, "Magic ear!"

"My God!" Old Gough-Bags looks like she's going to have a stroke and her hat almost flies off her head. "I can't believe I've just remembered that, and I can't believe you've kept that for so long!"

"Okay," Matt says, "my memory has gotten ridiculous over the years. I'm one of these people who loses stuff when they learn new things."

Charlie turns to Matt and points a shaky finger at Leon's tin. "Remember my first day at Brooklands? The first person I interacted with?"

Matt sits back, tries to rewind over thirty years of his life, shrugs, clueless.

"The first person I spoke to was..."

Charlie begins but Matt's face whitens and he blurts out, "Leon! In the bike sheds! Me, Johnny and Shane were watching, thought you were going to be like all the other di- idiots and take the pi- mickey out of him, but you didn't. You did the magic trick. The sweet behind the ear."

Matt contemplates the toffee penny in the tin. "Surely that can't be the same one?"

Mrs O'Hara nods as Leon carefully closes the tin and places it back in his coat pocket.

Charlie is lost for words, is unable to prevent the tears that begin to stream down his face.

Leon stands up slowly, moving like a doddery old man, and puts his arms around him, something the child version of Leon would never have dreamt of doing due to physical sensory issues.

Charlie can feel the others' eyes on him but he can't help himself, the tears come out and he sobs like the frightened child he still is sometimes, in the arms of the only innocent person he has ever known.

Your Frightful Spirit Stayed

5.

Matt gets a round in whilst Charlie makes an absolute state of himself and spends ten minutes apologising for being an emotional wreck. He gives them a condensed version of the years they've missed out on, tells them about his wife and son, shows them photos.

They all do the same, Matt doesn't mention any aspects of a private life, just academical and business successes. Charlie wonders whether his hints at homosexuality in their late teens flowered into something permanent.

Mrs O'Hara and Gough-Bags are deep into retirement.

Leon goes to some daycare centre five days a week and occasionally has holidays somewhere in the Peak District.

More drinks are drunk, Charlie takes up Matt's offer of sharing his hotel room, and then the whole night is ruined.

"So," Matt says, draining another designer lager, "what was the other thing in the tin, Leon?"

Leon doesn't answer, something they recall was a habit of his.

His mother answers for him. "It's a conker from that tree in Goswell's Wood."

Leon looks at the two men, sullen. "Now you see him, now you don't."

Charlie is swamped by the flashback that takes him across the decades to a secluded area where five boys stand over a hole in the ground.

Inside the hole lays a body striped with stab wounds and slashes.

Charlie is the one who throws the first handfuls of dirt over the corpse's face, not for any reason other than to cover up the death glare and stop their friend with Down's Syndrome from making a weird mewling noise they've never heard him make before.

"Now you see him," Leon says, now the ghastly visage is partially hidden by his friend's magic, *"now you don't."*

Matt starts pushing soil into the hole; it kind of carries on from there.

"Are you okay?" Mrs O'Hara lays a hand on Charlie's knee as she voices her concern.

The old Gough-Bag has mysteriously vanished; Charlie catches a slither of her pastel suit on the other side of the pub.

"Yeah," he says, but he won't look at Matt, doesn't want to see whether he remembers too. "Nostalgia overload."

Mrs O'Hara nods as though she understands but there's no way she can.

Charlie feels the anxiety flood through him like icy black radiation, there's nothing he can do to stop his head from hanging.

"God, I'm just really, really tired." He gives an unconvincing laugh and wonders why people do that at awkward times.

"I don't think alcohol agrees with me anymore."

Am I still talking to Leon's mum?

He isn't sure.

The black depths of his half-pint of Guinness look like they want to engulf him. He puts the glass down and feels it start to begin, stronger than ever before. *Ghostly visitation, full-blown PTSD panic attack, schizophrenic episode?*

Call it what you will, either way, he is surrounded by the smell and the very essence of that man. It's as if he's there with them at the table, sitting in Gough-Bag's now vacant seat.

Finally, he sees Matt's face, it's as pale as he imagines his own must be. He picks at his bottle label and taps one foot repeatedly against the floorboards.

Leon clutches his little tin tightly through his coat pocket with one hand whilst he wipes slug trails up his sleeve with the other.

Mrs O'Hara notices and reaches into her handbag for tissues.

The liquorice smell intensifies.

Matt's foot-tapping quickens, exactly in time with Charlie's pulse rate.

There is static in the air.

"Now you see him," Leon whispers, staring in absolute horror at the empty chair before he cries out and slaps a hand to his head.

6.

Everyone has left apart from Charlie and Matt. The sobs and the Guinness come out of Charlie in violent bursts as he sits at the bus stop outside the pub.

The paramedics pronounce Leon dead when they arrive, suspect it may have been a brain haemorrhage. Mrs O'Hara is devastated but relieved as if released from a terrifically long burden. It is she who offers Charlie comfort as they help her to the ambulance. She presses Leon's trinket tin into his palm, puts her arms around him, and he fails again by crying.

"It's okay, Charlie. Leon hasn't been well for years. He's had violent fits and nightmares since he was a teenager." She pauses, touches his cheek like a mother. "They took a little more of him each time, like he was slowly vanishing." She wipes her eyes and takes in both he and Matt. "But I'm glad he got to see you pair one last time."

"He's never going to let us go, is he?"

When Matt says this, Charlie stops crying. He knows exactly who Matt means but needs him to say it.

"Duncan."

It's barely audible over the wind and the rain when he does say it but Charlie hears it nonetheless.

"It's one of the reasons I came back," Matt says, and points to a red car in the pub car park.

Charlie shrugs.

"I'm going to dig him up and burn him. Maybe he'll give me peace, then."

Charlie laughs. "You're joking?"

Matt recoils angrily, "Don't you fucking laugh at me, you cunt! You don't know what I've been through because of that bastard."

Charlie opens his mouth to protest, to say that his laughter was involuntary, relief that someone else shared his horror.

"Fucking twenty-five years of drug abuse, rehab and fucking repeat, because that cunt won't leave me the fuck alone!" Matt rants and jogs in the direction of his car.

"Wait!" Charlie says, and follows.

Matt is in the car by the time Charlie catches up. Charlie gets in the passenger side without an invite. "I've pretty much had the same shit."

Matt bursts into tears and slams his head into the steering wheel.

He looks up at Charlie in the darkness, "he won't leave me alone," he taps his temple with a finger, "in here."

Charlie nods and puts an arm around him. "I know, mate. I know."

"I've considered owning up," Matt says, and Charlie feels cold but knows he's thought the same thing over and over again. "But I never wanted to incriminate the rest of you."

"I don't know what to say."

"That cunt has ruined all our lives." This time, Matt punches the steering wheel. "Even after all these years."

Charlie squeezes his shoulder.

"I've got everything we need in the boot," Matt says robotically.

"It'll be impossible to find it now."

Charlie doesn't want to go back to Goswell's Wood.

"I'll be able to find it, don't worry about that."

"Mate, it won't work, the weather..."

"I've got petrol, for fuck's sake. If you won't come, I'll do it on my own."

Matt starts the ignition.

"Matt, Jesus, he's not a fucking ghost! There's no such thing! It's in our fucking heads, don't you get that? This won't do shit!"

"It will give me closure." Matt pauses, hits the wipers and slips the car into first. "If not, it'll give me the bollocks to finally top myself and do the fucking job properly this time. Now you can either come with me or I'll drop you off at your parents on the way."

"Oh well, if those are the options, I'll happily come with you to dig up and burn a dead body!"

Charlie spits it out so deadpan, so unexpectedly, that they both start to laugh.

They drive towards Goswell's Wood.

Your Frightful Spirit Stayed

7.

The wind is whipping seven shades of shit out of the trees as Matt drives them down a dark country road towards St Michael's Church.

The roads haven't changed for decades, they are bumpy and treacherous at the best of times and the rain is falling faster than the wipers can sluice it away.

"Well," Charlie says, as Matt fights with the steering wheel, "we've picked a nice night for our reunion." He can feel the wind buffering the car even with the shelter from the high hedgerows; loose debris flies past the windscreen.

"I'll park by the church." Matt's stony, and in no mood for Charlie's gallows humour.

The headlights pick out a red hut that strikes unwelcome familiarity within Charlie, the Sunday school hut where he would be dragged to jumble sales and other tedious events.

Nothing changes in villages, he thinks, about Mrs O'Hara and old Gough-Bags, *not even the people.*

He wonders what happened to his other old friend, Shane Colbert, whether he really did know what happened to Johnny and his friends in the eighties and whether somebody in this time-forgotten place acted upon their twenty-year-old vendetta when he returned for his mother's funeral.

This village was the perfect location for a horror story and he had first-hand experience that real life was far more horrific than fiction.

Matt pulls in behind the Sunday-school hut and reaches behind Charlie's seat for his coat. "Come on."

Charlie puts a hand on Matt's wrist before it leaves the steering wheel. "Are you sure about this?"

Matt sighs, "it's something I feel like I've got to do. This will be the kill or the cure, I know it."

Charlie is petrified but knows no one will be out in this weather and the chances of even finding the location of the body is slim. They get out of the car; Matt unloads the boot.

The walk to the woods is imprinted in their minds even though neither man has trodden it for decades.

There are no changes, it could be any time in the last sixty years.

Charlie finds comfort in the sound of barking; he had forgotten all about the kennels at the rectory that lay behind the church; the dogs' voices used to carry all around the village on a calm night. He would listen to them as he tried to go to sleep. It was good to know they were still here. In the child part of his mind, they are the same dogs he remembers seeing through the field gate as they passed the graveyard years ago: a gigantic breed like a fluffy white wolf, and a pair of black Labradors.

The guardians of the village.

They pass the gate now, but he can't see onto the land to see if they're the same dogs.

Charlie carries a spade and walks behind Matt, who leads the way with a torch and a three-litre bottle of petrol.

The hoods on their raincoats are fastened as tight as possible, only allowing room for vision, but they are soaked by the time they reach the entrance to Goswell's Wood.

8.

It's only because they know where the entrance was that they can find it.

It's overgrown; forgotten.

The church path still slices that part of the village, a cut that's never allowed to heal.

They wring their ankles and scratch the backs of their hands fighting their way in.

Goswell's Wood doesn't want them back; it trips them and whips them with low-hanging branches and brambles and every step—like their lives since leaving this place—is a struggle of both body and soul. The shell of the house is still standing but only half remains.

Matt shines his torch around the walls and sees the bricks are now charred; their tree, with its prize-winning conkers, is a dead black thing that reaches skyward.

"Arson or lightning strike, do you reckon?" Matt shouts above the gale.

Charlie doesn't answer, just stares at the mess of rubble and ruin. There's no way they will be able to find where they buried him. He doubts they could find the spot during daylight.

Charlie watches Matt's torch beam crisscross the foliage and knows they've come on a wild goose chase. Matt knows it, too; his scream is more ferocious than the wind.

Charlie reaches to him and Matt lashes out with his hand.

The torch smashes against Charlie's face and he falls into deep, wet mulch.

Charlie tastes blood as he spits leaves and other stuff.

He is frightened, disorientated, cold, and doesn't know where he is.

It's dark and he knows, just knows, he's somewhere horrible, back in that place with *him*.

He's done something to him, to his face.

Everything else has been a dream, his whole fucking life.

He never left.

His fingers squish through the mud and he can't see—but he can hear *him* breathing above the wind and the rain.

Hear *him*, smell *him*.

Charlie tries to stand, and that's when he feels *him* pin him down, hands on his shoulders, pulling at him, at his clothes. When he opens his mouth to scream, more stuff blows in and his jaw hurts.

Charlie is hauled to his feet by someone a lot stronger than he is.

He feels something in his hand.

A wooden handle.

"Charlie!" The voice says, and it's not *him*, not who he thought it was, but it takes too long for him to recognise his own name and he's already swinging the spade.

Charlie uses the light on his phone to find out who he's killed, even though he already knows.

Matt lies on the leaves, the side of his skull bashed in; there's a brief flutter of life in his eyes and he says something Charlie can't hear, but which he can lipread.

Don't leave me here with him.
Then he dies.

Charlie collapses to the ground beside his last friend and through tears that will never truly stop, begins to scrabble away at the foliage to get to the soil below.

Ignoring his friend's dying wish and damning himself a little bit more, he starts to dig.

9.

After what seems like years, he gets back home, creeping like a mouse.

It's too early for anyone to be awake but he hears hushed voices.

He needs a shower, needs to wash his clothes, but more than anything he needs to fall into the arms of the woman he idolises and for her to make all the hurt go away. Again.

The door to their bedroom is half-open; he sees his best friend, Adam, slowly making love to his wife.

She looks so happy.

Charlie turns silently and heads back out of the front door.

Matthew Cash

*I remain, painfully connected to you,
you won't disappear or fade away,
touching, hurting, continuing to torture me,
unable to dismiss and make you untrue*

Your Frightful Spirit Stayed

Beth

1.

The first time it happens isn't long after Brantham is struck by tragedy. Charlie and his friends have drifted apart since that fateful afternoon in Goswell's Wood.

Matt had moved to Manchester when his father got the offer of a huge pay rise, Leon went to wherever people like him go when school is over, and as for Shane and Johnny, that was where the village tragedy came into play.

Charlie spends more and more time at home.

Michael has moved down to the bottom of the village into the flat above the chip shop with the girl who used to live next door to them, so he now has his own room to fester in.

It is good having his own space but he misses endless rambles around the countryside. It's hard going outside.

He can't bring himself to go near the places he and his friends used to hang out.

They drifted apart.

There are ghosts on every corner.

Shane splits his time between college, a job in some meat-packing factory, and a new circle of friends Charlie doesn't fit in with.

Shane still hung around with Johnny, though.

That pair had always been inseparable.

Until that night. The night Shane went out with a group of his new friends and something happened. Four of his friends vanished, leaving Shane in a coma.

Charlie read about it in the local paper.

He regrets shutting himself off from everyone, turning reclusive and not being part of the gang.

Shane came out of his coma with only one or two minor physical effects but total memory loss of that night. A lot of people think he is hiding something, that the group was in trouble with some heavies in town. Bit off more than they could chew. They did frequent some pubs of ill repute.

Charlie sees Shane for the first time in over a year, must be a few months since he has been let out of the hospital. From where Charlie perches in the armchair in his bedroom, he watches the double-decker bus pull up at the stop outside his house, the top deck level with his window. He sees Shane leaning against the glass, green mohawk spiked up over his head. He has lost a lot of weight and looks pale, ill.
Charlie turns away before he is seen.

It saddens him to know that he lives in the same village as three of his best friends and how time slowly passes without seeing them, as if the afternoon in the woods had driven a stake into the heart of their friendship.

Charlie slumps into a thick, depressive fugue, spends most of his days in his room listening to the mixtapes his brother makes him: heavy rock and metal.
Loud, screaming music that seems to somehow give him peace, but not enough of it.

His parents don't know what is wrong with him.

His mum suspects it is something to do with what happened in the past but he denies it when questioned.

Once a fortnight, he forces himself to leave the house to sign on, and lie to people in suits about how he has been looking in the newspaper for work.

Charlie knows there is something wrong with him, the burning anxiety he gets whenever he is due to leave the house.

It isn't normal.

He doesn't know what he is frightened of, why he seeks refuge in his room.

It feels like the only safe place left.

In his world, anyway.

It is after one of his excursions to the dole office that even that is taken away.

He comes in, briefly grunting at his mother. His father, as ever, is working, so he goes straight to his room to listen to Helloween as loud as he can get away with.

The smell hits him as soon as he opens the door, a combination of liquorice and sweat. It smells like *him*, like Duncan.

Charlie reasons there has to be an explanation; his mother has tidied whilst he has been out.

Despite him always telling her not to.

She's used a new brand of air freshener. A new fragrance. Or maybe she has been cooking something unfamiliar and the aroma has seeped into each of the rooms. But as he slings his bag onto his bed, the smell wafts from the unkempt sheets. Angry that something has sparked off unwanted memories, Charlie stomps across the bedroom, the floorboards shuddering, and lifts the ancient sash window.

The air from outside blows chilly into the room.

Though the sun blazes onto the road, summer's ferocious beast is giving way to autumn's creeping, aged miser.

Charlie drops into the threadbare armchair and sticks his feet on the windowsill. He flicks the play button on his cassette player as though he hates the thing and is trying to dislodge an eye.

Screaming guitars shriek around his room, shortly followed by the slapping of his mother's palm against the glossy painted wall of the staircase below.

"Fuck's sake," he growls, and jumps out of the chair to retrieve his headphones from his bag. The smell hasn't abated and when he bends to unzip his bag it is as if he has dunked himself into an icy pool.

Charlie freezes as his head is engulfed by the strong odours of sweat and liquorice; wisps of breath unfurl from between his chattering teeth.

"Can you turn it down, please? I have been shouting," Mum snaps from the open doorway, one hand on the doorknob, the other screwing up a wad of the apron she always wears around the house.

"Sorry," Charlie mutters, and is as surprised as his mum by the unusual lack of venom in his voice. He moves away from his bed and turns the volume down completely on the cassette player.

"I didn't say you couldn't..."

"Mum, can you smell that?"

Mum smirks incredulously, "Now, come on, I'm not falling for that one anymore."

Charlie shakes his head and points down to his bed. "No, it smells funny, like someone's been in here—" He hesitates—as though what he's about to say is taboo. "—And of liquorice."

Mum frowns, immediately strides across the room, and thrusts her face towards the bedsheets. "I can't smell anything other than the musty smell of your stale farts and the fact your sheets probably need a change and you a bath."

Charlie shrugs; the smell is still too obvious to him. "It just smells weird and feels a bit cold."

Mum points to the open window, "Close that, I'll strip your bed off and you go and grab a can of air freshener."

With that, she yanks the sheets down.

Charlie turns to leave the room.

"Oh, for Christ's sake!" Mum spits.

She holds aloft one of the sheets: two pea-sized holes have burned straight through.

"If you're going to be selfish enough to smoke in the bloody house after I've told you time and time again not to, at least try not to burn the place down."

Charlie stares at the singed, black holes.

He hasn't smoked in weeks.

2.

By the time his mum has changed his bedsheets and sprayed enough air freshener around the room to asphyxiate an elephant, the cold spot and the smell have finally gone.

As the evening draws in, he wonders about things that he often nightmared about as a child: silly things, impossible things, supernatural things, things he used to frighten himself with before he discovered real things to be scared of.

He never believed in ghosts and stuff; it was ridiculous, even the concept. Surely if there were such a thing, it would have been scientifically proven by now.

Everything has an explanation.

People only live on in other people, in memories or physical imprints they leave whilst alive. Pieces of people left inside other people. He gazes down at the quiet road below him, the light from behind him casting his own distorted shadow on the tarmac. It is monstrous from this angle; a spindly-limbed giant made of night.

He stares hard at the shadow's head, where the eyes should be, and wonders which pieces of which people have been left behind in him.

As a kid, not long after they moved to Brantham, he and his brother watched what he could only describe as a Disney horror film, *The Watcher in The Woods,* and it scared the hell out of him. Bette Davis plays a scary reclusive guest house owner who becomes obsessed with the newly arrived neighbour's daughter, as she resembles her own, lost child.

Much of the movie's plot has faded in his memory, but the key scenes that played havoc with his imagination are as clear as ever.

The pretty, blonde-haired protagonist entering a Hall of Mirrors alone, the close-ups of her gleaming face laughing at the quirky distorted images before finding herself in the ever-perplexing mirror maze, more close-ups of her even, white teeth — then the smile falters; a look of terror as she watches the myriad versions of herself turn into glimpses of Bette Davis's daughter. The silent spectre reaches out towards her from every reflection, arms outstretched, begging, her lips clearly asking for help, and to make the scene even more surreal, a dirty, ragged blindfold covers her eyes.

Watching that film instilled a phobia of mirrors in him. Each night, he would flash frightened glances at the foot of his bed where the white wardrobe stood, looking at his frightened face peeping over his blankets, half-expecting, dreading the gradual appearance of a wispy apparition in the full-length mirror.

A recurrent nightmare, which added to the other stresses of the upheaval of getting used to a new life, was when he had fallen asleep without noticing, and in his dream, he was still in bed. He would perform his ludicrous, compulsive routine of checking the mirror every few minutes only to freeze at the sight of a man's sinister, laughing face wavering in the space above his bed. The clink of the magnetic catch as the mirrored door depressed itself and slowly creaked open, the dark gap expanding, revealing the real monster inside.

He would wake everyone up, screaming from a wet bed.

He presses his face against the glass in the window, not so frightened of his reflection anymore but still not entirely comfortable with looking into mirrors. His reflection always seems to scrutinise, a different entity altogether, as though it were the only thing that was aware of what has happened and what he has done.

Your Frightful Spirit Stayed

3.

He goes to sleep that night with thoughts of wayward spirits with unfinished business, the unpleasant nostalgia of resurrected childhood nightmares, and wakes in the darkness, freezing cold with noises behind his headboard.

Charlie's instinctive reaction is to look down to the foot of his bed at the window. For a second he is expecting the old white wardrobe to still be standing beside it, but is happy to just see his tapes. The window is closed but still his teeth chatter. When he sits up to pull the quilt over himself, he catches a whiff of that same familiar aroma, sweat and liquorice, and lies back down quickly.

A rustling comes from the wall behind the headboard; he shoots out of bed and thunders across the room to switch the light on.

There is nothing to see anywhere in the room, let alone the corner where his bed is, but he can feel something electrical in the air. The hairs on his arms stand rigid; goose pimples freckle his exposed skin. He steps over the creaking floorboards and over to his bed and gingerly pulls the headboard away from the wall. The bolts that attach the headboard to the bed have gouged great holes through the textured wallpaper into the plaster. As he moves the board away, the plaster crumbles, making the same noise he thinks he heard upon waking.

Behind the head of his bed, behind the headboard, beneath the plaster and wallpaper, is what his dad suspects was a door. His parents' bedroom is adjacent to his, with a narrow staircase separating the two rooms.

When the house was built, both of the bedrooms had a walk-in wardrobe joined by a small partition that spanned the stairs below. His dad assumed that one of the previous occupants had blocked it up in what they referred to as the front room, knocked through the partition, and made the master bedroom closet bigger.

Charlie marvelled at the idea of blocked doorways, excited by the prospect that there might be part of the place he had not yet discovered.

Maybe they hadn't knocked two cupboards into one, maybe there were some buried secrets, a hidden area?

When he was younger and they had not been living there long, Mum said that if he needed her at night to knock on that door, as it was pretty much audible over the whole house.

The powdered plaster trickles down the wall. Charlie digs his index finger into the hole the bolt has made and feels a change in texture as his skin touches wood.

Once again, the smell of liquorice and sweat engulfs him, and he thinks he hears someone whisper behind his right shoulder.

Charlie spins around, his heart bursting out of his throat, the tip of his nose pressed into an Arctic cold spot. The strange but familiar odour increases in strength and for a few seconds he sees white wisps of breath curl before his eyes.

"Whaa?" He yells out and presses himself against the headboard. The smell gains intensity, it stings his eyes, forces him to squeeze them tight, something on the boundaries of his hearing whispers his name, and Charlie's scream wakes the whole house.

4.

Charlie sits in the doctor's surgery surrounded by sniffling kids and tutting old people who scowl resentfully at anyone who doesn't appear to be on the brink of death.

He feels stupid sitting beside his mum amongst the coughs, colds, sciatica, and God-only-knows-what ailing those around him, a time-waster.

The patients sit around the edge of the room, holding plastic cards with numbers drawn on in black marker pen, all eyes either at their feet or the small grey box above the doorway with the doctors' names on, waiting for the orange bulb beside it to light and buzz dully to signify the next appointment.

Charlie pushes his index finger through the half-inch sized hole in his appointment card and spins it around nervously, fidgeting.

"Don't do that, you'll take someone's eye out if that comes off," his mother whispers harshly, and snatches the card off him.

Charlie rolls his eyes and waits for the ominous buzz. It comes too soon. A cold wave of nausea swamps his stomach. He looks at his mum pleasingly but follows when she stands up and hooks his card on a small rack on the wall.

Doctor Marshall is the only other person who knows about Charlie's past.

As soon as he murmurs stuff about hearing things that aren't there, the doctor stirs the embers of that fire.

"What happened to you as a child will likely stay with you forever, Charlie," says Dr Marshall, a Scotsman far from his native country.

He asks more questions about these unusual occurrences, in particular: the smells, their link with his childhood, and how he mentions his mood being low, says things that go way over Charlie's head.

Other words stick with him, though, break through the mumbling doctor's monologue, quicken his pulse, chill his heart. Words like Post Traumatic Stress Disorder and the one that makes his mum gasp out loud and thrust a hand over her mouth: *schizophrenia*. Further tests will be required, counselling is suggested, with the possibility of prescribed medication.

The walk back home is a blur of greens and browns as Charlie focuses inwardly on the paranoid fantasies of straitjackets and being thrown in the loony bin.

5.

Over the following months, his moods worsen and the hallucinations are in perfect synchrony with the lowest of these times. Counselling helps at first but there are things Charlie just can't talk about to anyone, even to the people who know.

Within a year of that fated doctor's appointment, medication is prescribed and the word *schizophrenia* is mentioned more and more.

Charlie feels himself sink into a numb world; a comforting routine.

The medication the doctor hands him not only shuts out the hallucinations, but also shuts out everything else, leaving him emotionless. He piles on weight; no food satisfies the emptiness inside.

It isn't until his mother intervenes and physically forces him into a daily schedule that Charlie's life starts to begin again.

The months spent in the fog of heavy medication have left him tired and unable to concentrate on anything for long periods but she can't see her youngest child rot away.

He becomes her dogsbody, her helper, unwillingly at first, until he finds himself actively reading the job adverts in the local paper and catching up with news of his favourite bands in the magazines he has ignored for months.

His social life also died that day in Goswell's wood, and now, after months of mental withdrawal, he doesn't even know where to begin to rebuild that.

That day was also the last time he saw Matt. He has his friend's number, they all have each other's numbers, but the thought of picking up the telephone makes his throat close.

The disappearance of the boys from the village is all anyone speaks about; all eyes and fingers still point to Shane, and while a large part of Charlie aches to reach out to his remaining friend, a bigger portion wants to retain his lethargic anonymity.

He finds solace in the pages of the music magazines he flicks through.

The back pages run ads for gigs and lists of merchandise for independent sellers of music-related paraphernalia. Alongside these, there are a few columns devoted to personal ads, musicians wanted, instruments for sale, and people who want to write to other, like-minded people.

Something called pen-palling. Something he knows without the shadow of a doubt that his friends (when he still had them) would have ridiculed him for.

It isn't the way normal people go about meeting other people, it isn't the normal way boys go about meeting girls.

Even Charlie thinks it is sad, that the kids seeking friends are likely abnormal, freaks, other loners like him, social pariahs. But despite selfish misgivings, he admits that he now fits into that category.

It feels strange to put pen to paper to write something other than endless jobcentre forms. He writes about who he was, not the person he has become over the last year, the fat, depressive schizoid loner who hears things that aren't there. He tells them about the interests he had before his downfall, and in a way, it helps him remember who he was.

Over the months, when the people he writes to become regular pen-pals, it becomes therapeutic. These people who share similar interests mostly do have reasons for choosing this method of socialising, whether it be confidence issues due to appearance, disability or poor mental health, and they spill their hearts onto the pages in multi-coloured blood. It is through this medium of correspondence that he meets Beth.

Your Frightful Spirit Stayed

6.

Charlie is the first off the coach; he almost slips on the steps. His whole body trembles with fear, he tries to close his eyes and breathe for a moment, but there are so many people. As soon as he stops, someone pushes him out of the way.

He scans the station signs, sees one for the toilets, and rushes to it. Everything is a blur of too-fast movement aside from the blackened doorway that heralds his salvation.

He shoulder-barges the door open, startling a person coming out. He tries to offer an apology to the angry-looking man, but even speech is hard. He slides across wet tiles to the closest cubicle, locks it, and vomits into the toilet bowl. Nothing much comes up aside from the water he drank on the coach; he has been too nervous to eat. Now he has finally achieved what he never thought possible, he feels he will die.

A six-toned beep chirrups from his pocket, his stomach finishes spasming, he spins around, and sits down on the toilet seat. He takes out his Phillips and presses the unlock button; the aerial has come loose again in his pocket. He twists it on tighter.

The message is from Beth, *Im @ stn. Its fkn freezin. Is yr coach l8?*

Charlie grits his teeth and holds back tears. This is everything he has been waiting for. He is here, and he is almost certain he is going to bottle it completely.

The tears come; the crushing anxiety explodes along with the air from his lungs and the toilet roll holder he has been clutching.

There is nothing else for it, he will ignore the text, stay in the toilets until Beth goes home, and use his return ticket to go home on the next available coach.

His heart aches for what he was going to be sacrificing. The love of a girl he has never met. The love of someone he has only seen in photographs. The love of someone he already idolised.

She liked obscure, uncool bands and films and books and didn't give a fuck.

He even loved her handwriting, the long tails she would put on the hoops of her lowercase h's and m's.

That she seemed to even write with an accent.

That whenever she wrote his name, she would draw a heart around it.

He even carried a photocopy of the photo she had sent him in his wallet as though she were his real girlfriend.

He's spent hours looking at that photo; her pale skin was so striking, a contrast to her pink lips and her blue-grey eyes. She looked Nordic, elfin; she wasn't smiling but there was a twinkle in her eyes that suggested she was capable of mischief.

Charlie feels the loss of all that, of all that he had had, of all that he might have had, as he sits crying on that toilet, his mobile phone chirping every few minutes with texts from the girl of his dreams. And then, as if to make the agony worse, he notices it when he bends forward to retch between his knees: the slight tang of liquorice.

"No, no, not here!" He mewls through phlegm-speckled lips. It has been weeks since he has experienced one of his hallucinations—the meds saw most of them off—but now he is at his lowest, he is having one.

The smell becomes stronger and Charlie screws his eyes closed as the familiar tang wafts under the cubicle door.

"Please!" Charlie prays to the cubicle door; his voice comes out way louder than expected. Someone hammers on the other side.

"You alright in there?"

The voice is male, accent thick, northern.

"Yeah," Charlie manages to croak, notices the smell has gone.

"You gonna be long? The other bog's bust."

Charlie finds himself standing, automatically yanking the chain and reaching for the lock.

A fat man in a National Express uniform stands on the other side of the door. "Cheers, mucker, sorry to rush you, like, but I'm due on in five."

Charlie nods, passes by the man and stops in front of the mirrors. He has made his mind up to be a wimp, hide out in the toilets until Beth has gone, and regret it for the rest of his life. An icy blast of air hits him as another man rushes into the gents. His reaction is to look towards the newcomer, to the open door—and that is when he sees her.

And she sees him.

As the door swings slowly shut, he sees her wave.

7.

The anxiety increases tenfold.

He can hear the blood rushing in his ears and feels his stomach being squeezed by an imaginary fist. The dark side of the exit door beats in time with his rapid pulse; his breath comes with difficulty.

She has seen him.

Charlie's shaking hands rest on the cold door. He hears a toilet flush, shuffles of feet behind him, someone clearing their throat.

He is in the way.

He wants to die. Wants the building to collapse on him. Anything to avoid this.

The door opens slowly, as if the person entering the men's was unsure or incapacitated in some way. "You coming out, mate? cuz I don't really like hanging around the bloke's loos." She sounds different than he'd imagined, her voice is throatier and louder than expected.

Charlie feels the presence of someone behind him, knows he has no other choice than to open the door.

Everything seems too bright when that door opens, even though the day beyond is dull, lifeless, and freezing.

He stares in what must be absolute horror at the short, skinny girl in the bobble hat. Her pale face is cracked into a crooked grin that crinkles her nose and makes light glint off the stud that pricks her left nostril. "You look scared shitless, mate!" Her laughter, which he hopes isn't directed at him, is mischievous, infectious, she is the epitome of cute—and he has already fucked everything up.

Charlie moves his lips to say something - anything, but he is still in the toilet entrance and someone pushes past him.

"It's okay to be nervous, mate," Beth says, her grin fading, and those blue-grey eyes that seem too big for her face, too old for her face, bore into him with such intensity that he can't tear his own away. He feels her slender fingers curl around his shaking, sweating palm. "It's alright, come on." A softer smile then, one of comforting reassurance.

Charlie lets himself be led away by the girl of his dreams, into the dank confines of the coach station.

8.

She sits him down at a table by a window in the coach station café and walks over to a service counter. The interior is vast, cheap, and not much warmer than outside; condensation clouds the glass, blurring the world beyond. Charlie stares at her; he is still the petrified, rigid rabbit facing oncoming headlights, but a small flicker of hormonal craving begins to surface when he checks out the rear of her flared jeans. He quickly pulls his eyes away when he feels the beginnings of a more physical arousal.

His mind is a kaleidoscope of things he wants to say and be in front of her, but he has not yet uttered a single syllable.

He thinks about the pages and pages of A4 they had sent each other week after week, full of everything they had been doing, every little thought and feeling.

Diary entries for only one other reader.

They have both said *I love you*, weeks ago, before the trip was planned. Beth has even written stuff about wanting to do stuff with him: cuddling, kissing, touching, *fucking*.

Charlie's cheeks flush as Beth starts back with two polystyrene cups in her hands and several sugar sachets held between her lips. A smirk finds its way to his mouth and he hears her chuckling as she approaches.

"What are you grinning at?" she says after she opens her mouth and lets the sugar fall onto the table.

Charlie shrugs, the stupid grin, the embarrassment, going nowhere.

"Gotcha tea, I remembered you like tea," Beth says, pointing at one of the cups as she sits down opposite him, "but I don't think we ever discussed how we take it." It is her turn to look sheepish as her grin widens and her pale cheeks darken. "We kinda had other stuff to talk about."

"I'm..." Charlie forces the words out without thinking, without even knowing what he is going to say, "... I'm glad you came and got me."

Beth smiles, reaches across the table to take his hand, and whispers, "I'm glad I came and got you, too." She squeezes his fingers but doesn't let go. Her eyelids flutter and she lets out a nervous laugh, "I haven't been able to eat all day, my stomach's felt like it's been inside a giant's fist. I've been nervous and excited and it's been just so random, but now you're here, I could eat a fucking horse!"

It both shocks and comforts him that she too has been nervous about their meeting, normalising her. He begins to feel the earlier overwhelming anxiety fritter away in this curious girl's company. Charlie spots the familiar golden arches of one of the world's most popular food franchises through the rain-blurred window. "There's a McDonald's over there, I don't think they specialise in horse meat, but I promise I'll buy you the biggest burger on the menu."

9.

She is joy, she is sunlight embodied, her smile thaws out the cold, hollow spaces inside of him he thought frozen forever, and ignites fires he never knew burned.

She makes him feel again.

She teaches him how to live, how to love.

His trips to see Beth become as frequent as each of them can afford.

She will take every shift McDonald's offers her outside of her college hours and give him purpose.

He pines through the long days between visits, always listening out for the bleep of his mobile phone.

Once a month, more often if time and money allow, they meet for a whole weekend and they show their love physically.

Feverish and hungry, they devour one another alive and long for a time when they can be together, forever.

Unlike a lot of other relationships, the notion of moving in together is discussed seriously. This is where the first arguments begin.

Arguments with his brother Michael, about not running away with the first bird who opens her legs.

Arguments about where to live.

Both Beth and Charlie want to move away from their home towns, Beth through the sheer mundanity of living there for nineteen years, and Charlie for deeper, darker reasons.

Reasons he won't go into.

It has been hard but he tells her about the schizophrenia, the unusual hallucinations that haunt him, but she accepts it nonetheless.

He can deny Beth nothing. He idolises her, and, albeit reluctantly, he agrees they will search for a flat in his local town.

It will be far enough away from Goswell's Wood so he won't have to go there, but not so far that he can't see his brother and parents regularly.

Charlie rises through positions in a number of retail outlets until he eventually becomes a manager.

They get comfortable in a spacious flat.

They get pregnant and they are happy.

It is short-lived.

Goswell's Wood: Death

1.

Charlie checks his watch and carries his bike across the foliage on the woodland floor.

It is fucking cold out; he wonders whether the others will show up.

They better had, seeing as it was their idea.

Shane was the one to tell him, Matt gave him a note, told him to pass on the info at school. Charlie is willing to bet any amount of his secret stash of fags he has at home that it is girl trouble.

Shane, though geeky, seems to be popular with the girls at school. Matt was always bragging about this and that, but no one could disprove his stories as he went to a different school.

Charlie lays his bike down and stomps over to an area amongst the trees where the remnants of the Goswell cottage shed lie. The rusted corrugated sheeting provides the shelter to what they call The Pit.

He is the first to arrive, as ever.

He pulls at one of the iron sheets and makes a gap just big enough for him to slip down into a hole in the ground. Fumbling in his haversack, he takes out one of his detachable cycle lights and switches it on, illuminating the dark confines. The familiar rotten smell of filthy old hessian potato sacks is comforting. He rests the cycle lamp on a thick loop of tree root that they carefully dug around years before, and lights up a cigarette.

Charlie has always liked the pit; it is his special place. Somewhere he can relax and think.

Often he comes here without the others, it seems to be happening more and more.

Shane and Johnny had always been a double act since he met them, Matt was too sporty for his liking, even though he was a good mate. The others had their hobbies and interests, Matt's fucking football and fucking scouts, and Shane and Johnny's bloody comic books.

Charlie doesn't mind his own company, has learned to get used to it after the fucking fiasco of the last day of primary and the embarrassment that leaked over into high school.

He isn't surprised that he never told anyone about what happened at The Flower House. According to his parents, it was a subject best forgotten. But sometimes it eats away at him. Sickening flashbacks that can be ignited by a smell or a phrase, or *that* fucking song.

When Frannie Wilkinson tried to kiss him at the school disco, he reacted badly. For the rest of his life, he would regret pushing her away, and remember the look of shock and hurt on her face as she fell onto her arse, spilling punch all over her white top.

She was pretty — *fuck*, she was beautiful, everyone thought so, even he did, but it was always enough for him just to sit and talk with her. He wasn't like other boys his age, obsessed with the opposite sex.

Obsessed with sex.

The cooler kids in his year were forever bragging about sexual shenanigans they had reputedly gotten up to, or girls they wanted to bang. He had been happy just talking to Frannie.

But that hadn't happened since he'd reacted like that to her attempted kiss.

He had been tarred with the homo brush and the latest rumour was that he was gay and having an affair with Johnny.

Normal fifteen-year-old boys would not turn down the likes of Frannie Wilkinson.

There had to be something wrong with him.

"I'm a fucking idiot, that's what," Charlie growls, stubs his cigarette out on the skin of his inner forearm, wincing at the pain but happy that it has driven back the tears that threatened to surface.

The last thing he wants is for the boys to get here and take the piss because he has been crying.

Speak of the devil, he thinks, as he hears voices in the distance, and feels a bit excluded when he realises the others were all together. He lights up another fag and pulls out the four-pack of beer he's nicked from his dad's shed.

Half of the corrugated sheeting slides across as Shane and Johnny come into view. "Fucking hell, what you doing down there in the dark, having a wank?" Shane says, grinning down at him.

"No, man, I ruined that photo of your sister, didn't I?" Charlie fires back and blows smoke in his face.

"You wish, mate, Cathy wouldn't touch you with a barge pole," Shane says, and drops into the hole beside him.

"I'd touch her with my pole," Charlie says, and punches his friend in the arm. "Wanna beer?"

Shane's eyes light up, "Whoa, man, how the hell did you get them?"

Charlie shrugs and nods to Johnny, who appears to be lost amongst the pages of something sci-fi. "Nicked 'em off me dad, didn't I? He'll just blame Mike."

"Charlie!" comes a voice he hasn't heard since the last school holiday.

Charlie squints up into the daylight and sees Leon, his ever-present smile beaming down at him. "Leon, my main man, come on down," Charlie says, jumping up with genuine glee and offering a hand to his friend.

Leon looks nervously at the remaining corrugated sheet covering half of the pit's opening.

Charlie pushes it out of the way, "Sorry, mate, I forgot." He reaches down and grabs his cycle lamp. "Here, you can have a play with this." He flicks the switch back and forth a few times, making the red lamp shine.

Leon nods and climbs down into the pit and sits cross-legged on the ground. Johnny perches on the rim, trainers dangling down, still engrossed in his comic.

"Where's Matt?" Charlie says to Shane as they both sit back and crack a can.

Shane shrugs. "Dunno, probably got the bus, didn't he?"

Charlie smirks and nods across to Leon, "Can't believe you brought the dude here."

"Ah, well, we thought you'd need cheering up after all that shit at school this past week."

"Fucking dickheads, they are." Charlie swallows some of the disgusting-tasting beer.

"Dickheads," Leon says, absentmindedly flicking Charlie's light on and off.

The boys chuckle.

"Don't say that to your mum, Leon," Charlie says, stifling the laughter before turning back to Shane. "Was his mum alright with it?"

"Course, man, she trusts us, don't she? We've been taking him out on our own since we were kids, man. Plus, I think it gets a little bit difficult since *you-know-what* happened." Shane whispers the last four words.

It is common knowledge about Leon's father dropping dead of a massive heart attack, but the last thing they want to do is mention it in front of Leon. Although they don't think the boy fully grasps the concept of his father's death, neither wants to hear the repetitive questions that would follow if he was reminded.

"Who the fuck's that?" Johnny suddenly blurts out from above them, staring at something out of sight. He turns his head down into the hole at the three boys, his long, greasy hair obscuring his crooked grin, "Fucking Matt's brought his dad or something."

None of them have met Matt's parents and are surprised that the one member of the gang who thinks he is the coolest would embarrass himself by bringing along his mum or dad.

The prospect of an approaching adult makes Shane and Charlie immediately put out their cigarettes and hide the beer cans back in Charlie's bag.

Charlie wafts his hand through the air to dispel smoke that isn't there and wonders if the guy is this Keith bloke who Matt has been harping on about recently.

"Alright, John," he hears Matt say before he steps into view of the pit, roll-up cigarette in his mouth.

"Alright, you lot?" he says, sounding like that comedian off the telly as he peers into the hole. "Come up here and meet Keith."

Charlie rolls his eyes at Shane, a secret message that he is annoyed, and nudges him with an elbow. He doesn't mix well with strangers, and from what Matt has been saying about this Keith, he sounds dodgy. Letting him smoke and drink, actively encouraging it, buying it for him and his mates from the town school. Until he saw Matt up there with a fag hanging out of his gob, he hadn't believed him.

Charlie is in no rush to meet the bloke so he pushes Shane and Leon up first.

As the two other boys climb up, Shane first so he can help Leon, Charlie hears Matt introduce Keith to them one-by-one as they emerge from the pit.

"Keith, this is Johnny, the tall one is Shane, this is Leon, the one I've been telling you about, and somewhere down there is Charlie."

Charlie hears the grunts of *hello* from his friends, and the polite, "Hello, I'm Leon O'Hara, do you like magic?" He puts a foot onto a step they've dug into the wall of the pit and begins to push himself up as Keith speaks.

"Alright, guys."

Charlie freezes; his heart leaps into his throat.

That voice.

It is the first time he has heard that accent around here aside from his parents. Not many people from the West Midlands end up here. He pushes himself up out of the hole and sees his friends standing with a hooded figure.

"Alright?" Charlie says uneasily, nodding toward the bloke.

The man returns his nod and grins.

His face is half-hidden by the shade of the hood of the camouflage raincoat he wears, but Charlie thinks it is because of a strange birthmark blemishing the skin around his mouth.

An awkward silence befalls the group as they stand in the woods with this man, a man known to none of them but Matt. Matt seems to sense it and knows that it is up to him to get the conversation going, seeing as he's the one who's brought Keith along. "Err, Keith's a mechanic, aren't you?"

"That's right," Keith says, and gives a small laugh.

Charlie's instinctive feeling of unease slowly intensifies.

What is the guy doing here?

He is way too old to be hanging around with them; he is old enough to be their dad.

"Keith's fixing me up a car for when I'm old enough to drive and he's already given me some lessons, haven't you?" Matt says, smirking at Shane and Johnny's impressed gasps. Leon stands beside Charlie, smile plastered on his face, mind far away, probably reliving some magical theatrics he had seen on television.

"You don't recognise me, do you?" Keith says to Charlie.

A cold bolt of fear paralyses him.

The man throws back his hood and laughs at the boys' horrified reactions.

"Hey, you idiots, it's not funny. He nearly died in a car crash!" Matt shouts, defending his friend from any potential ridicule.

It reminds them of Freddy Krueger from the Nightmare film they saw the poster of in the video shop. Keith's head is covered in thick scar tissue, only one side of his jaw clear of any damage. Charlie mutters something unintelligible and steps back towards the pit.

"Careful you don't fall in, Jacob," Keith says slowly.

"*Charlie*, his name's Charlie," Matt says, wondering what is going on.

Charlie skirts around the hole ignoring his friends' confused patter, he instantly feels the piss running down his legs and the years of his attempts at burying his past disappear. He runs around the wide hole and stumbles across the corrugated sheeting.

"Stop!" Keith shouts, and Charlie would have ignored him if it wasn't for his friends' frightened cries.

Charlie twists and sees Shane and Johnny huddled together.

Johnny is beginning to cry, Shane's face ashen, Leon has his hands plastered to his ears and his eyes screwed shut, an instinctive reaction whenever someone raises their voice.

Keith has his arm around Matt's throat, pressing a huge fishing knife against the curve of his jaw bone.

Matt looks frightened, cheated, confused.

Charlie stands on the corrugated iron, the wide aperture of the pit between him and the man of his nightmares.

"Now, you come on over here, Jakey," Keith says, his voice thick with menace, "and I'll let the rest of your little bumchums go."

Charlie wants to run. To run and never look back, but he finds his feet shuffling across the rusted sheets and foliage towards the scarred man. Tremors which seem to radiate from his heart shake his whole body; speech won't be possible with the fear he feels. All he can see are his friends' frightened faces and the sharp crescent of the knife pressing against the golden tan of Matt's throat.

Will Duncan kill him, or will it be the same as before?

He stops halfway around the pit, fear overriding his movements.

Maybe if we all run at once?

He looks at Leon, who is fine now the shouting has stopped, his hands wedged in his trouser pockets, his perpetual grin back in place while he shuffles his feet on the ground and mutters to himself.

"Let them go." The words that leave his mouth are a lot braver than he expected.

"Ho ho, Jakey boy has grown some bollocks," Keith says, as he shoves Matt onto the ground and grabs Charlie by his school shirt collar.

Matt rolls across the ground and is instantly helped up by the ashen-faced Shane and the trembling Johnny.

"Now fuck off, you lot, me and Jacob here have got a lot of things to catch up on," Keith says, twisting Charlie's school tie around in his hand. Johnny's red eyes plead with Charlie for forgiveness a second before he flees through the trees.

"I'm sorry," Shane says, his eyes welling up, and follows Johnny.

Matt shoots Keith a look of heartbroken denial, scrabbles about on his hands and knees, gets to his feet, and hurries after his two friends.

Keith looks at Leon with a bemused smile on his face, "Piss off, Quasimodo."

Leon completely ignores him.

"Please," Charlie says, whimpering, "leave him alone."

Keith laughs dryly; the thick scar tissue on his face barely moves.

"Nah, nah, three's company, in my book." He yanks on Charlie's shirt and tie, dragging him across the ground towards Leon. "What the fucking hell are you supposed to be?" Keith says, hissing with laughter.

Leon mutters something to himself and grins.

"What did you say?" Keith prods him in the chest, knife still in hand.

"Please, leave him alone, he's got Down's syndrome, his name is Leon, please—he doesn't understand."

Charlie clutches at Keith's coat sleeve, tears spilling onto the waterproof material.

"He can speak for himself." Keith pokes Leon hard enough to make the boy step back.

Finally, he makes eye contact.

"What's your name?" Keith spits.

Leon smiles his usual smile: warm, friendly, welcoming, "My name is Leon O'Hara, do you believe in magic?"

Keith laughs again.

Charlie thinks back to the time Leon introduced himself to Stuart Gant, the new kid in Mrs Hazelwood's class at primary school. How the kid laughed when Leon greeted him the same way.

The slap Leon had bestowed upon his cheek in response.

The red handprint, the immediate swelling.

God knows what Duncan would do if he slapped him like that.

He imagines the man's knife plunging into his friend's chest and knows he has to intervene before it's too late. "Say 'yes'," Charlie splutters.

Keith sniggers at the weird-looking boy with the streamers of snot wetting his upper lip. "You fucking mong. No, no, I *don't* believe in magic, you little pri—"

The slap comes out of nowhere and Charlie's heart stops.

The schoolroom slap had been bad, for a nine-year-old, but now Leon was near twice that age, twice as strong.

The swipe is unexpected, at least as far as Keith/Duncan is concerned.

Leon strikes the unblemished side of his face, sending spittle from his mouth, blood from his nose, and the knife from his hand.

Keith loses grip of Charlie's shirt collar, his face slackened by the shock. Anger soon flares up; he reaches for Charlie once again.

Shane comes out of nowhere. So does the branch he swings around like a baseball bat into Keith's face before he has a chance to recover from Leon's blow. An angry roar comes from his left and Matt shoves him towards the pit.

Silence befalls the group, Shane drops the wood, Matt bends, his hands clenching his knees as he retches onto the dirt.

Johnny appears out of nowhere and runs to Leon's side. Charlie joins him.

Moans come from the pit.
Together, they move near the rim.

Keith lies at the bottom, bleeding from his nose and forehead, and his left leg is bent the wrong way. A shard of bone pokes through the material of his jeans, ghost-white against the murk of the den. "Help, you need to call an ambulance. I won't tell on you, I swear. It was an accident." Keith blurts the words between agonised moans.

Charlie stares down at the man; he looks pathetic, nothing to be feared.

He feels someone brush against his shoulder, Charlie notices the golden complexion of Matt's skin.

"He," the boy speaks, his usual bravado absent from his voice, "he did stuff to me."

Just five words ignite an undiscovered rage inside Charlie. He has heard the term '*seeing red*' before on the cop dramas his dad watches but has never experienced it first-hand.

The anger and hatred seems to flow from inside and out through his eyes, mouth, and hands.

Before he becomes aware of what he is doing, he lands knee-first on Duncan's stomach, winding him and causing a silently scream.

A flash of silver is in his hand and it is the only time he is aware of the knife before he plunges it downwards, opening a red groove in the side of Duncan's neck.

Blind rage guides his hand, the strokes and slashes a blur as he mentally relives the things the man did and the things he might do — the things he might do again and again and again.

Shane is brave enough to climb down the hole, and put his arms around Charlie. He whispers into his ear, his breath a warm breeze, "Stop it, mate, please."

Charlie breaks out of his trance and recoils at the mess he has made. His wet, red hands shake in front of his face, he flinches when he sees the knife and drops it to the soil. He falls backwards and pushes himself away from Duncan's massacred body, refusing to believe he is capable of something like this.

Matt jumps down, landing in a crouch beside him, and helps Shane haul him to his feet, but not before aiming a thick wad of phlegm at the dead man's ruined face. "Cunt."

The four of them sit on the edge of the pit. The dead body below has lost most of its shock value now they have looked at it long enough.

Leon sits further behind, back to his musings and mumblings.

"I first saw him hanging around by the shops here," Matt says, staring blankly into the hole, "then I saw him outside my school in town. I thought it was weird to see him there again in such a short space of time but figured he'd got a kid going there, you know, like me?

"Then me and one of the lads I hung about with from the sixth form were on about going into the town to see if we could get served in The Falcon. We didn't," Matt laughs bitterly, "Well, *I* didn't. So, I walked off to the bus station in a sulk. That's where I saw him again. He started talking to me, he seemed alright, told me he had been in a fire back where he used to live, that he had saved a family. I think because his accent was the same as yours, I believed him, trusted him." Matt leans on Charlie. "He told me he was a mechanic, he bought me booze and fags, said it was what being a lad was all about. Started asking me about girlfriends and such, what I'd done, what I hadn't done. One night he invited me to his flat in Ipswich for a takeaway and a booze-up. He—" Matt rubs at his eyes, "—he forced himself on me. Stuck his prick inside me." He breathes out and stops wiping away the tears.

He ignores Shane and Johnny's groans of disgust and continues his story. "The next day he was so sorry, spent a hundred quid on me just like that. Told me he was going to fix me up a car, kept buying me stuff."

Charlie forces himself to swallow the lump in his throat; hearing Matt say those things is far from easy.

He stares at the dangling feet of his three friends, begins his own story.

Matthew Cash

*Jesus Christ keeps on turning his head away,
even though the beast most foul has now died,
he couldn't save me in my hour of need,
I must remind him of this failure every day.*

Your Frightful Spirit Stayed

Matthew Cash

Goswell's Wood

1.

At least it's another village, Jacob thinks, as his dad drives past a black sign with the place's name on. His parents have already been living there a week, they have taken all their worldly possessions and set up home in the new house.

Mum says the village is just like where they came from, although a bit more peaceful. Dad has secured himself a job at a factory nearby and he and his brother have got places at the local schools.

They pass a freaky little modern church that looks like a converted redbrick house, as if they just swapped the normal windows for stained glass ones.

Jacob always finds churches creepy.

Rows of semi-detached houses line both sides of the main road, old houses stuck together in pairs, most of them seem to be colour-coordinated with their neighbours'.

His father flicks the car's left indicator and pulls up into a driveway. Jacob looks up at the houses, they are all named after ladies, and called *villas*. Decorative plaques high up beneath the eaves tell them that their new house is called Edith Villas, that it was built in 1900.

"See, I told you it was nice," his mother says, unfastening her seat belt.

Jacob takes in the two-storey house with its tiny front yard, and smiles glumly.

A flash of yellow hair speeds up the side of the detached neighbouring house and a young teenage girl comes rolling out of the passageway on brightly-coloured roller skates. Her long bare legs dance in the sunlight as she steers her way down the footpath.

Jacob sees his older brother stare open-mouthed at the retreating girl. He catches Dad smirking in the rearview mirror at Michael. "What do you think, Mikey?"

"Err," Mikey says, his voice coming out as a pathetic squeak. He clears his throat and sounds more normal, "Yeah, yeah, looks alright." He quickly fumbles with the door latch.

"Oh, Mike?" Dad calls to his flustered firstborn, "her name is Kelly and she'll be in the same year as you at school."

Jacob surprises himself by smiling at his brother's panic-stricken expression.

The house is smaller than their old one, even though it has the same number of bedrooms. Mum has already unpacked everything whilst Dad has decorated whatever needed decorating.

It feels weird walking into a building he's never set foot in before and seeing the familiar items from their old home. The first thing he notices at the top of the looming stairs is the horrible painting that used to hang behind the sofa; he wishes it had been left behind.

"Come on, I'll show you around," Mum says, switching on a light and trotting up the dimly-lit stairs.

The ceiling above the steps looks miles away, goes up at a dark and gloomy right angle where the low wattage light bulb can't penetrate. A square hatch sits directly over the small landing at the top of the stairs; Jacob stares at it dubiously, their old house didn't have an attic. A sense of foreboding comes from the dark, unfamiliar corners.

He and his brother follow their mother as she takes them below the attic hatch to show them her and their dad's bedroom. Nothing majorly exciting except for the view out of the window over a long but narrow back garden, houses and trees beyond, the view of the neighbour's lawn.

"What's in there?" Mikey says, nodding to a door on the far wall. A small door leads to a little empty box room.

"Another bedroom. I guess they would have used it as a nursery, seeing as it's joined to this one and so tiny." Mum opens the door and shows them the little room. "You see—not much good for anything. Dad's hoping that one day we can turn it into another toilet or bathroom."

Michael surveys their parents' room and the small one connecting. "You should let us have this room and turn the little one into a games room."

Mum gives Michael a disapproving shake of her head and ignores his suggestion. "Right, let me show you guys your room. I've tried to lay it out the same as it was back in the old—" she pauses and lowers her eyes, the word already on her lips, "—*home*, but you pair can chop and change as you wish."

Before Jacob or Michael can start reminiscing or whining about the house and the life they have left behind, she treads across the room, over the landing, and opens their bedroom door. "Dad has put in a surprise for you. It was his idea, but you pair take the mickey and I'll move it downstairs."

She leads them into a brightly-lit, blue-painted room; aside from the stuff from their old bedroom, they spot the 24-inch television and hi-fi system beside it.

"Whoa!" Michael cries out in disbelief, "but you always said..."

"Yeah, well, it's a new start for all of us, I thought it would be nice for you and Jakey."

Jacob fakes a smile; it is nice, the room is nice, bright, the window overlooks the quiet main road, with a windowsill wide enough to sit on—which is wicked—and the room is almost the same size and shape as their old one.

But it isn't their old room, Grandma and Granddad Carter can't come round every Friday night to babysit and kiss him goodnight.

They are far away from them.

Having a telly is good, Mum always said they couldn't have one in their room before, but he knows Mikey would be the boss of it because he is the oldest. To prove this point, his gangly teenage brother flops down onto the bed with the WWF duvet cover and flicks the TV on.

"*...with me down Diamond Drive...*" The comedian sings, dancing along the rainy cobblestone. Jacob feels his bladder release the huge amount of urine he hasn't had the opportunity to purge after the long journey. It takes Mum and Michael a few seconds to register why he is shaking and sobbing, and to notice the spreading wet patch on his tracksuit bottoms.

"Oh Jesus, Mike, it's that program, turn it off!" Mum shouts, and wraps her arms around his quivering little brother.

Jacob cries into his mother's shoulder as Michael flicks the switch off.

"It's okay, baby," Mum says, stroking his mousy hair, "that evil man is far, far away."

Jacob knows it's true, but hearing that song brings him straight back, the sound of his harsh, excited breathing, and his smell: liquorice, tobacco, and sweat.

2.

The school looks a lot smaller than his previous one, with a single storey. The grey-bricked building sits nestled at the bottom of a grassy hill that separates it from a small road and a row of modern houses. Hordes of children jostle about on the concrete expanse that is the playground, smaller groups stand beneath the low roof of a long, creosoted bike shed. Jacob casts a wary eye towards his mum, who squeezes his hand and smiles reassuringly.

"It'll be fine, Charlie," she says, his second name still foreign on her lips, "a new start."

Jacob clutches the strap of his rucksack tightly, "Did you tell them about...?" he leaves the sentence unfinished; she knows the rest.

"No," she says quietly, "they don't need to know about it unless anything happens."

Jacob shoots her a frightened glance.

"Not that it will!" his mum hastens to add, before she bends down, pecks him on the cheek, and gently pushes him towards the playground.

As he joins the writhing melee of children, a few close by stop mid-play and stare. Jacob nods at them and gives a slight grin. Expressions of vague interest soon change back to excitement at whatever game they have been playing.

They were looking because he is the new kid; it is better than the looks he received from the people back home. His old friends, their mothers especially, had gazed upon him—after the newspaper had made it clear what had happened to him—with a look he never wanted to see again.

The kids wanted to speak to him, to ask him questions, but they were told not to go prying.

It had been hard, those last few weeks, seeing the kids he had grown up with avoiding him or treating him differently for fear that they would not be able to resist asking him about what had happened.

Maybe things will be better here, he thinks. He can't find much to fault about the village and the people he has met so far, and Mikey is already smitten with the girl next door. Jacob casually walks past a group of six lads kicking a ball about and retreats beneath the shelter of the bike shed.

A little boy in a blue anorak stands in the corner chatting to himself, his hood is pulled up tight around his odd-shaped face. Big blue eyes flit at Jacob for a millisecond before he wipes a sleeve of his coat across his nose, drawing two silver slug trails onto the fabric.

Jacob smiles and immediately knows it was the same kind of look his old friends had given him, one full of sorrow and pity.

This little kid doesn't need that.

It was obvious just by looking at him he was what they called 'special'. They had a special class at his old school, some kids used to tease them and laugh at them but Jacob never did, he knew they couldn't help being different.

"Hi," Jacob says, raising a hand to the other little boy, and steps closer.

The boy's indecipherable incessant chattering stops momentarily and in a voice that sounds too deep and posh, says, "Hello," before he carries on mumbling to himself.

"My name is Ja..." He stops abruptly. He isn't Jacob anymore, not even Jakey. Even though he, his brother and their folks had been given new surnames when they moved, he was the only one who had been made to change his first name.

"My name is Charlie," he says, officially putting his former self behind lock and key. He is Charlie now.

The kid opposite him beams at him ecstatically before continuing to mutter.

Charlie leans back against one of the wooden posts holding the bike shelter up and watches the kids in the playground whilst catching the odd intelligible word or phrase from the special kid.

"You'll like it, but not a lot, hey presto!" He says, amongst a padding of gibberish, and slowly makes his way closer to where Charlie stands.

Charlie feigns disinterest and soon feels the other kid's finger tap him on the shoulder.

He turns around to face the special kid.

"Leon," the boy says in his posh voice, and prods himself in the chest with a proud smile. "Leon O'Hara."

Charlie smiles and turns back to watching the other children; he notices a group of three boys huddled together looking his way. Apprehension begins to flower up inside him, he doesn't like their conspiratorial glances.

As they approach, Leon O'Hara taps him on the shoulder. His pinched features screw up into another big grin, the corners of his mouth nearly meet his smiling eyes. "Like magic?"

Charlie hesitates. If these other kids are as he suspects, will seeing the new kid mingling with one of the kids from the special class taint him in their eyes before he's even started the first day?

He sheepishly nods at Leon; he can't very well not talk to him just because he is worried about what others may think. "Yeah, yeah, I watch Paul Daniels now and then."

Leon nods enthusiastically and holds both of his hands out, palms up. "Magic."

Charlie watches as Leon rolls up each of his snot-streaked sleeves and shows that there is nothing in his hands. "In my hand," he shouts theatrically, waving and pointing his left hand over his right palm, "is a shiny red telephone."

Giggles nearby don't draw Charlie's attention from Leon's magic trick.

The weird kid freezes, hand poised over the other as though waiting for a response.

There is nothing in his hand but Charlie has enough sense to humour the lad. He nods in reply, not confident that a verbal answer will be possible without laughing.

Leon claps his hands together, brings his closed fist to his lips, and blows it, covering Charlie with spittle.

He slowly uncurls his fingers. "Look," he whispers dramatically, "it's gone!"

Charlie nods and claps twice. He can't help but feel endeared to him even though he is one of the special kids. He eyes the three approaching lads and ignores their sniggers.

"Do you want to see a magic trick, Leon?" Charlie asks, subtly rummaging in his pockets.

Leon nods excitedly.

Charlie shoots his hand up behind Leon's head and magically produces the sweet he secreted in his palm, and is horrified when the boy flinches and falls to the ground with his hands covering himself. He wails as though Charlie has just struck him. The playground falls silent, a stern-looking teacher strides across the concrete, a metal whistle poised between her teeth.

Charlie crouches down to the shaking child and tries to say something to comfort him. He pinches the sweet by one of its cellophane twists and dangles it in front of Leon's face. "Magic. Magic sweet from behind your ear."

Leon's crying stops as abruptly as it began and his eyes go wide in wonder. A quivering hand gently plucks the shiny gold-wrapped bonbon from Charlie's fingers and he stares at it, enraptured by the magical offering.

"Magic," Charlie says, smiling, as the heels of the approaching teacher's shoes scrape across the ground.

Leon gingerly touches his own ear and beams up at Charlie like he is some kind of Messiah.

"Excuse me," the teacher says in a snooty voice that makes her sound like the Queen, "Leon is special, he doesn't like being..."

Charlie offers Leon his hand and the boy willingly takes it and allows Charlie to help him to his feet.

"...touched," the teacher says in astonishment as Charlie smiles at Leon, turns to the teacher and the silenced playground, feeling the blood rushing to his face.

Leon laughs, brings his hand up to Charlie's ear and miraculously produces the same sweet from behind it. "Magic ear."

Charlie blushes, but sparked by the glory of his improvised performance, decides an encore will make a solid impression on everyone watching.

He flicks his hand back up to Leon's ear, knows he is taking a big risk with how the boy reacted before, and magics a blue sweet. He drops it into Leon's other hand, amused by his surprise.

Leon's face changes from bewildered to a broad expression of pride as he swiftly pockets the sweets and points at Charlie. "Friends. Charlie and Leon O'Hara."

The teacher's severity softens as she allows the unusual act of kindness this new boy has made surface.

"Hello, I'm Mrs Gough, welcome to Brooklands School."

3.

After Mrs Gough blows on the metal whistle, the children rush into orderly queues behind specific numbers painted on the playground floor.

Charlie remembers he will be in Class 6 and after saying goodbye to Leon, he sadly ambles towards a smaller line of students on the far side of the expanse.

The three boys who witnessed his interaction with Leon make sure they are behind him in the line. As the teacher calls out the numbers in a seemingly random order, a boy nudges him in the shoulder.

This is where the teasing starts, thinks Charlie; there was a stigma at his old school about talking to the kids from the special class, no reason to think it would be any different here. He turns his head slightly to the boy behind him.

"I'm Shane," the boy says. He's a tall kid, almost a foot taller than anyone else in the line, and stick-thin. "That was cool what you did with Leon, gimme five." He offers Charlie his palm.

Charlie smirks a little shyly and slaps the tall boy's hand. "Cheers, I'm Charlie."

A little rat-faced boy pokes his head around the tall boy's shoulder and smiles awkwardly exposing jutting, bucked front teeth. "Hi, I'm Johnny, pleased to meet you."

Another boy pokes his head around the other side of the tall boy, chubby-faced with a halo of white-blonde hair, "Alright, I'm Matt."

4.

Life at Brooklands erupts from that day onwards: for once, he is the cool kid, his first impressions in the playground that morning having instilled a newfound burst of confidence.

A new start, a new life, no more Jacob. Jacob is gone, dead and buried along with his past and his previous nightmares.

Charlie is a cool kid; his surprising entry to the small village primary school, his tolerance and affection for someone less able than him soon sets an example amongst the other children.

No longer do the children from the special class stand at the edge of the playground, clinging desperately to the teaching assistant's hands, excluded by the other children. They are accepted by the others, following the new boy's example.

Charlie is the popular kid, with his strange accent, modern ways, and this confident new persona that has somehow miraculously manifested itself.

The new grey uniform is like a superhero costume, symbolising his new identity.

But at home, when he sees his family, the memories return. In between numerous glassy-eyed daydreams over the girl next door, his brother Michael always casts a wary eye over him when he mentions going out to play with his new friends. That look, the momentary shadows that pass over his parents' faces before they fake smiles and tell him what time to be back.

The distraught rush to the television set if that program comes on, and the slapped hands over mouths and nervous glances when they use his old name, hoping nobody's heard their mistake.

Home is the place where he can't forget.

Unfortunately, Charlie's status as the coolest kid in class is short-lived and comes to an abrupt end on the last-but-one day of term before the much-anticipated summer holidays.

It has been a blistering hot afternoon and in Mrs Hazelwood's class, the kids are getting lethargic after playing in the sun at lunch break.

Straight after break there has been a drama when a few of the better-behaved children from the special class came in to do some art with them.

They have been reading The BFG as a class for the past few weeks, and to commemorate the brilliant story, Charlie has been painting a picture of one of the nasty giants destroying a building.

Leon instantly comes and sits beside him when his teacher brings him and Mark Rogers from the special class in. He is doing his usual attempts at art. He isn't very keen on getting messy, doesn't tend to like wet stuff on his skin, so he gingerly dabs the tip of the brush in and out of the paint pallet and presses the bristles hard against his paper to watch as they splay.

Stuart Gant, a new, geeky-looking kid whose parents have moved from Scotland, is at their table, and he keeps smirking at Leon, obviously amused by his disabilities.

Charlie doesn't like the new kid much, not just because he has stolen his limelight as the cool new kid but because he comes across as a bully.

He is outspoken and instantly popular, good at sports, too.

He begins to fire questions at Leon without really understanding that the boy usually never pays any attention unless you say his name, and rarely speaks to anyone first. Charlie can see he is getting wound up at being ignored and thinks he will help by explaining that he only responds if you say his name. Stuart looks at him as though he is just as different as Leon and pulls a face before turning once more to the object of his amusement. "Oi, what's your name?" Stuart blurts out, jumping up out of his chair as Leon stands up to go and wash a speck of red paint from his hand.

Leon beams at the boy, his trademark greeting whenever he is asked this question. "My name is Leon O'Hara. Do you believe in magic?"

Stuart laughs in his face as if hearing Leon speak was the funniest thing he has ever heard, "No, of course I don't!"

Leon's hand strikes out so quick it's barely visible, but the noise is heard around the class. Everyone is silent and stares at Charlie's table at the two standing boys. A red handprint flares up on Stuart Gant's cheek; he bursts into tears. Leon's shocked teaching assistant rushes across the classroom after helping with the other special kid, and the grandmotherly Mrs Hazelwood leads a bawling Stuart from the room.

After all the commotion and the whispering has settled, Leon and his classmate go back to the static mobile classroom whilst Mrs Hazelwood gets one of the caretakers to bring the TV across. Having the telly in the classroom is always an event. The huge wooden set is wheeled in on a portable, metal-framed shelving unit, and rolled squeaking across the room, wires looped on top of the video recorder.

Mrs Hazelwood thanks the caretaker and sets about unravelling the coils and plugging it in. She spends the next five minutes trying to figure out how to get the infernal device to do as she wants. But today, she is wise to the fact that where modern technology is concerned, she is useless, so calls upon a member of the class to sort it out for her.

Shane is the willful volunteer and runs to the front of the room to fathom it out. After a few minutes of tinkering, he stares perplexed at the snowy screen. "I don't know what's wrong with it," he mumbles with embarrassment.

The little lady does the same thing Shane's just done , her face a concentrated wrinkle.

Charlie thrusts his arm up in the air, his hand writhing like a dancing cobra.

"Yes, Charlie, if you know how to set this up so we can play the video, please come on up." Mrs Hazelwood folds her arms, stepping back.

Charlie leaps off the floor away from the other cross-legged children and vanishes behind the TV set.

He pulls and swaps some of the cables behind the box and video recorder.

"I hope you know what you're doing, Charlie," Mrs Hazelwood says, as though simply fiddling with the input and output wires will cause the thing to blow up.

"Yeah, Miss, the caretaker has put the aerial in the wrong..." Charlie begins but is drowned out by the children's sudden outburst at the images appearing on the screen—followed by a twinkling music box melody with backing piano and the sound of heavy rain.

Charlie stops, feels the warmth around his crotch, and before he has even realised he has wet himself, golden trickles run from beneath his shorts and onto the carpet.

The man on the TV, that curly-haired comedian Diddy Dave Diamond, starts singing. He, too, is drowned out by incessant laughter as the children finally spot Charlie and his ever-increasing puddle.

5.

Luckily for Charlie, the village is a paradise for children to grow up in, the summer of his arrival is blisteringly hot, seems never-ending, and for the first time, he has three friends living close by. Despite the horrendous incident on the penultimate day of term, the friends he has made remain loyal. These things happen and people soon forget, like the time Robert Cousins fainted and hung across his chair upside-down, arms out like Superman flying, glasses askew. Something else will happen to someone else and it will be their turn for ridicule.

Every day, the four boys are straight out after breakfast, racing around on their bikes.

The village is located at the top of a hill and descends into a deep valley that turns into marshland along the River Stour.

The main populated areas are surrounded by farmland and rolling fields of wheat. Footpaths skirt the edges and weave between secluded ponds and up and down hills.

"Come on," Shane calls from up front, "let's show Chaz Goswell's Wood."

Johnny and Matt cheer and follow his lead. Charlie steers his bike towards the kerb, lifts his backside off the saddle, and bumps up onto the path. Shane rides over the grass and down a narrow pathway between two houses, ringing the bell on his handlebars to alert any unsuspecting pedestrians.

The path is only wide enough for them to ride single file. It winds down beside high wooden fences secreting back gardens, giving the occupants privacy from the public footpath but not obscuring their view of the picturesque fields and the river.

The perilously steep footpath stops abruptly, and the squeal of bicycle brakes shrieks throughout the valley. Charlie squeezes his handlebars tightly, turning his front wheel when he comes to a stop to avoid bumping Matt's back tyre. "Shit."

"Why have we stopped?" Matt shouts, dismounting his bike and wheeling it to a bend in the path.

Charlie gets off his BMX and follows Matt around the bend.

The path dips even lower to a miniscule footbridge where Shane has stopped, bike propped against a metal handrail. Johnny is already by his side, leaning his bike against a back garden fence.

Shane points down beneath the bridge at a pathetic tiddle of a stream trickling through a concrete pipe. "I once crawled through there for a dare!" he boldly proclaims.

Charlie leaves his bike on the ground and goes to inspect the site of Shane's heroic deed. The pipe is easily wide enough to crawl through and even though there are only a few metres where it vanishes beneath the field before it widens to slice the land in two, he doesn't fancy doing it himself. "Wicked," he says, praising the tall boy's bravado.

"There was a dead rat in there," Johnny says, hacking phlegm and spitting it into the shallow water. "Maggots and stuff wriggling out of it."

"Gross," Charlie says, and musters up a mouthful of saliva.

to add to the ritual. As Shane and Matt gave their offerings to the god of the stream, Johnny nudges Shane and grins crookedly, "'member when we blocked it?"

Shane's eyes go wide, he laughs, "Yeah, once, me, Johnny, Matt, and Christopher Moore came down here and we put loads of mud and dirt and stones and stuff in the tunnel and blocked it right up!"

Matt, feeling left out of the conversation, butts in with the punchline to their adventure, "Yeah, and the bloody stream flooded everywhere, the field, and," he says, pointing at the slatted fence, "that old lady's garden!"

"Whoa!" Charlie says; the scene he is picturing is a lot more dramatic than the reality had been. "Is that what we're going to do now?"

"No way, José," Shane says, and nods to the other side of the bridge. "I just stopped here so I could tell you about what we did, but mostly to give you the lay of the land and to warn you."

Charlie feels his confidence weaken. Have the past few weeks all been a joke? Was this where they told him they didn't like him?

"This path," Shane begins, staring dead seriously, tracing the slope they had just come down and pointing to the far side of the bridge, "is the most dangerous one in the village, especially when you're biking." He puts his arm around Charlie's shoulders and steers him across the bridge to a slight upward bend in the path.

"You see, the bridge over the stream is the Blind Spot and only people who are brave enough can keep pedalling when they come down this hill." He prods himself in the chest. "I pretty much do it every time I come here. But the whole challenge is to see if you can bike up the hill on the other side. And the only way it's possible is if you bike down like Billy-o and don't stop at the Blind Spot."

They turn the bend; Charlie is floored at how steep the hill is. "Bloody hell, it's a bloody mountain!"

Shane gazes up at the sunlit path that goes straight up; at its summit, the path continues alongside dense wood. "Fancy trying it tomorrow?"

Charlie nods excitedly.

"Come on, let's get the bikes and see how far we can get up before we have to jump off."

6.

Somehow they reach the summit of what the three boys call Church Path Hill. Charlie has never walked up anything as steep and the thought of biking up fills his head with images of tumbling head-over-heels, back down to the little stream.

The view at the top is spectacular. They can see more of the sparkling river a mile away, a brief snippet of the railway line that runs past the far edge of the fields, and a row of houses where civilisation starts again.

"You can see for miles," Charlie says, taking in the landscape of his new home.

"Yeah, 's alright," Shane says, shrugging at the scenery he has grown up with. "Come on, let me show you the woods."

At the top of Church Path Hill, the boys wheel their bikes through an uneven entrance into the woods.

Charlie is amazed at how dense the canopy of trees is; in the shade, the temperature change is immediate. Outside the woods, the sun was burning hot; he could feel the slap of sunburn on the back of his neck, so it feels good to be out of it for a while.

Shane stands his bike by the bulky trunk of an overturned tree and leans against the bark. "This is Goswell's Wood, we've been coming here for ages. No one else comes here at all."

"Charlie!" comes a voice from behind them, and discredits Shane's brag.

They turn and see Leon stumbling awkwardly into the woods, a portly middle-aged man walking behind him.

"Hey, Leon," Charlie says, greeting the boy with a pat on the back, "you alright?"

Leon ignores his question, something Charlie is used to, as it is often difficult to get his attention. "Magic ear?"

"Not now, Leon," The man behind him says, and then nods to Charlie. "So you're the famous Charlie we've been hearing about, are you?" He offers his hand out to Charlie, who reluctantly shakes it.

The man's palm is sweaty and he holds Charlie's hand longer than he is comfortable with; he snatches his hand away and wipes it on his shorts. Noticing the strange look he gets from the man, he disguises the hand wipe by subtly retrieving something from his pocket. The only thing he has in there is a few sticks of gum; he secretes one in his hand and does his magic trick with Leon.

The man chuckles at his son's expression of wonder as Charlie pulls the stick of gum from behind his right ear.

"Ah, so that explains where that came from," he says, and roars with laughter.

He turns to Shane, Johnny and Matt. "I know who you lot are, you alright lads? Hope you ain't getting up to any mischief, don't forget I'll no doubt be seeing your dads down The Crown this evening."

The three boys fumble about with awkward mutterings of, "No, Mr O'Hara,"; "We're always good,"; and, "Just taking a break from the sun."

"Ah, good, good. Well, we usually stop off near the church and have our sandwiches, and after walking up that ruddy hill, I'm ready for them." Mr O'Hara wipes a hand over his balding head and chuckles again, "Come on, Leon."

Leon flaps a hand at the boys and then follows his father back out the way they came.

Charlie frowns and turns to the others. "Why'd they come in the woods just to go back out?"

"Beats me," Shane shrugs. "Come on, let's go."

The gangly lad leads them through the woods along an overgrown track.

They walk for ten or twenty minutes along the pathway Shane chose, before Charlie notices something ahead through the trees. "What's that? A house?"

"Yeah, it's where we're going," Shane says.

"Who lives there?"

"No one now, it's derelict." Shane brushes past a spanning wire of bramble. "My dad said it used to be the old rectory, years ago, but there's a newer one closer to the church."

Charlie remembers seeing the square tower of the little church before they descended the hill towards the Church Path. He always finds them creepy, especially graveyards, all those dead people, and how no noises ever seem to penetrate them.

"There's a grave!" Johnny blurts out, nudging his way past Matt and walking beside Charlie. "By the house! There's a gravestone."

"Oh, not this again," Matt grumbles, trailing behind.

Shane laughs, "Go on, Johnny, tell him all about it."

Johnny sticks his middle finger up at Shane's back. "They're just trying to wind me up. They think my theory's shit."

"Which theory is that, then?" Charlie asks as the trees begin to clear, revealing a dilapidated house.

The roof is completely gone but it doesn't look like it has been through a fire, just age; brickwork is visible beneath the ancient white cladding. There are no windows, probably smashed decades before, and most of its useful materials seemed to have been gleaned from the carcass. It's pretty big, must have had at least four bedrooms. To the left sits a collapsed shed or chicken coop, nothing more than a pile of wood and rusted iron sheeting.

"Wait till you see inside, it's amazing," Shane says. Unable to contain his excitement, he runs ahead towards the yawning hole where a door once stood.

Charlie follows, surprised the house isn't covered in graffiti, most stuff like this would be. He doubts the boys' allegations that no one else comes into the woods, although there is very little evidence that anyone does. Maybe they thought it was too hard to get to, too overgrown.

At one point along the walk, they'd had to crawl through six feet of brambles. Charlie felt the scratches on his arms itch, and Shane had promised it would be worth it. When he follows him across the threshold of the house, he is taken aback.

The only thing intact about the house was its outer walls; remnants of the collapsed floors still cling to the sides, but it is well and truly open to the elements. A few rotting beams somehow manage to stay up, giving the impression of the shape the roof once took, like the stray strands of Leon's dad's comb-over. But the central point, filling up the whole interior, is a horse-chestnut tree. It appears to have grown where Charlie supposed the stairs would have been, billowing up into an explosion of green that has, over the years, burst through the house reaching for the sun. The branches are laden with white blossoms and budding green cases that will form shiny brown conkers. Shane smirks at Charlie's open-mouthed amazement. "Told you it was good. When autumn gets here, these are the best conkers in the village — once, I managed to get a twelver!"

"Wicked," Charlie says, imaging conkers as big as apples, as hard as a rock.

"Reigning conker champion of Brooklands two years running," Shane says, breathing on an invisible medal he pretends to have around his neck.

"Brilliant," Charlie says, awestruck, loving the way nature has claimed back this house. He guesses the tree is sheltered from the harsher elements, protected from gales and such, but the windows and roof let in loads of sunshine and rain.

It is so magical, he can almost believe it is a secret, that no one else knows about it.

"Look," Johnny says, pointing to a thick branch that reaches out towards one of the upstairs windows. An ancient green rope hangs from the branch.

"He reckons it was a noose," Matt says, swatting the rope out of the way as he picks his way across the interior.

"Betcha it was!" Johnny says. "Look, you can see where the rope snapped."

"It was probably a swing or something," says Shane, something he has said numerous times but repeats for their new member. "Johnny's a morbid git, thinks there are ghosts and stuff around here."

"There is, Dave Martin's sister says she saw a girl floating through the woods wearing an old-fashioned nightie," Johnny protests, and turns to Charlie with wide-eyes, "And she vanished into thin air!"

Matt sniggers, obviously sceptical to such fancies, "Dave Martin's sister is a fucking spaz."

"Why don't you show him the grave, Johnny? I know you're dying to." Shane clutches his belly and laughs, "Get it? *Dying to.*"

"Come on, follow me." Johnny walks towards the tree trunk and stands behind it. Charlie follows, noticing the others haven't bothered to join them.

The rear of the house isn't as intact as the front and sides; a vast amount of the brickwork has crumbled and fallen. Johnny goes through the remnants of a doorway and across the remainder of a small, cobbled path.

There is another collapsed shed or hut in the shade of the house. Ahead is a small clearing where the curved oblong of what looks to be a gravestone sticks out of the long grass.

The stone is ancient, green, crumbling; Charlie crouches down to inspect it. "Maybe it's part of an old building or something."

Johnny rolls his eyes and stamps his feet, "Oh, not you 'n'all." The boy is crestfallen, his theory once again pooh-poohed.

"Why would a grave be here when there's a churchyard nearby?" Charlie says, sitting down on the grass.

Johnny's eyes light up, "Ah well, now that's where my theory kicks in, see? St Michael's Church has been on that site for like one thousand years, right?"

Charlie shrugs.

"It has, says so on the leaflets in the foyer. Well, the village gets its name from the Anglo-Saxon words meaning 'burnt home' due to all the Viking raids in this area ages ago."

"Is this gonna be a history lesson?" Charlie groans and flops backwards onto the grass, the sun in his eyes.

"Ha ha, no. I'll cut it down a bit for thickos like you who just want the bums and tits of it," Johnny says, moving his head in line with the sun, giving him a halo.

"I reckon, judging by how old this stone is—" Johnny begins again.

"How old is the stone? How do you know how old it is?" Charlie quizzes.

"It's really, really old, look at it!" Johnny thrusts his finger towards it. "I reckon Goswell's Wood was planted on an old Viking burial ground."

Charlie thinks about it, about there being hundreds of skeletons below them wearing those helmets with the horns on. "Okay, that does sound cool, and a lot more interesting than it being part of an old building."

"See? I reckon there's something really important buried here beneath Goswell's Wood, and one day, I'm going to be the one to discover it," Johnny says, basking in the thought of future glory.

"So why don't we start digging now?" Charlie asks, surprising his friend.

"What?"

"Don't say you've not thought about it. We could find some gold or something."

The two boys race to suggest the idea to Shane and Matt, who have been taking it in turns to swing on the rope on the branch.

Despite much protest and mockery, they finally agree when Charlie suggests making a den by digging a hole and using some of the ruins to make a roof. It gives the four lads a summer-long project, something to occupy the six-week holiday, and they can simultaneously guard the prized conker tree in the process.

*Your legacy is very alive and real,
despite a broken body now slightly aged,
I'm fighting onward as always has been,
hoping to one day, to no longer feel.*

Your Frightful Spirit Stayed

The Flower House

1.

Come on, Superboy, you can do it! Jacob whispers to himself as his legs pump up and down faster than he ever thought imaginable.

It's a balmy summer day and he races towards the shops on his Grifter. It's black with cool spray-painted mud on it, and has thick tyres like a motorbike. It's a proper big-boy bike, it has six gears which you have to twist the handgrips to use.

Just like a real motorbike.

Every few seconds, Jacob risks taking a hand off the grip to check the fifty pence piece is still in his shorts pocket. Getting to the shop and finding out he'd lost his money is the worst nightmare this eight-year-old can think of. Fifty pence is loads.

He bumps down the kerb and shoots a glance both ways as he pedals like mad across the quiet road.

With his eyes on the prize, he squeezes the brakes, skids his back wheel in a semi-circle before jumping off his bike and running into the newsagents.

"Alright, Jakey? Pocket money day already?" says a fat old woman behind the counter.

"Hiya, Mrs Sutton, yeah it is," Jacob answers with a polite blush that blooms on his cheeks whenever an adult speaks to him.

He heads straight to the display of penny sweets, determined to get as many as he can for his money.

A few Blackjacks; though they taste a bit weird, he likes the way they make his tongue turn black.

Some cola bottles.

Loadsa cola bottles.

A couple of chocolate coins but not too many because they melt quick.

Once he fills the paper bag with supposedly fifty penny sweets (it's sixty-two, he lost count at thirty-eight), he hands the bag to Mrs Sutton for inspection.

She does her usual thing by peering wearily into the bag for a second before winking. "Yeah, that's fifty."

Jacob hands the lady his money.

"So, what are you going to do today? Apart from stuffing your face with sweeties?" Mrs Sutton smiles as she hands him his sweets.

Sweeties is such a baby word, Jacob thinks. He really should tell Mrs Sutton to call him Jake now, he isn't a baby anymore. He has been coming into the shop since he was born, though, and Mrs Sutton has always been there, so he figures he will let her off. "Gonna go play with Justin and Stuart."

"The Goodchild Twins?" she asks with raised eyebrows.

Jacob nods.

"They're little sods, that pair, I wish they'd live up to their surname."

The comment goes way over Jacob's head as he thanks her and leaves the shop.

He doesn't think his friends are little sods at all, they are cool.

His mum says they are spoiled rotten, though. They do seem to have everything they want, all the latest toys, and everything is always new and not an older brother's like most of his stuff.

Jacob stuffs a couple of the chocolate coins in his mouth and mounts his bike.

The sun is burning and his wristwatch tells him it is just midday. He bikes past the shop, holding on to his sweets with one hand.

Sometimes he is surprised at how good he is on his bike, only three years back he was using stabilizers and now he can do loadsa cool stuff.

He grips on to the handlebars, pulls a wheelie to get up onto the path, and instantly takes a left.

Jacob holds on tightly to his sweets as he bumps down a steep incline of shallow steps. When he reaches the bottom, he stops for more sweets, selecting a fruit salad chew to add to the chocolate spit in his mouth.

Sometimes he likes spitting on the ground after he's eaten chocolate and watching ants and stuff drown in it. He's very interested in insects; his favourites are ants and spiders.

Spiders are especially good, because—not that he will admit it to his friends—he's a little bit scared of them. He knows the twins are frightened, too, but they would never admit it, either. The Goodchilds have an excellent garden, a massive frog pond and loadsa bushes and stuff that crawls. They like catching bees and horse flies off the hedge and putting them in webs they find.

Jacob unwraps another fruit salad and drops the wrapper on the floor.

The best way to catch a bumblebee is with a clothes peg. You have to wait until the hedge is humming with the things then move slowly with the peg open. It's best to aim for a wing, as you wouldn't damage the bee that much.

Once you have caught it and made sure it is secure in the squeezed peg, pull its other wing off, that way it can't get away. Then you find the big spider web and throw the bee into it. You have to make sure it's a good web, though, because if it's too little and flimsy the bee will destroy it.

Jacob's favourite ones are the webs that look like little tunnels; you can almost guarantee a wicked big spider lives in them. The few seconds waiting to see if the web will hold the bee and, more importantly, whether or not the web is in current use, are nerve-wracking.

Then, there's that tiny shiver of fear and excitement mixed with morbid curiosity as the arachnid finally makes an appearance. The first step of the spider's first black leg as it appears in the tunnel is the best bit.

Jacob pedals beside the canal, watching dragonflies hover over the flowers on the lily pads. He'd love to be able to catch one of those, they are massive—but very quick.

A frightened little laugh comes out of his chewing mouth when he tries to imagine a spider big enough to catch one of those.

Almost as good as spiders are ants. Finding an ants' nest is even harder than finding spiderwebs.

Drop a maimed insect near the opening of one of those and it is brilliant. Once, he and the twins lay on their bellies watching as Stuart plucked both wings off a bee and dropped it on the entrance of a huge ants' nest. It was amazing how they attacked the bee in a group, biting and nipping at it with their tiny pincers.

It reminded Jacob of the films they used to show on a Sunday afternoon where a group of explorers or shipwrecked survivors would find a lost island where dinosaurs had somehow evaded extinction.

The bee was the dinosaur and the ants were the people trying their best to bring down the colossal creature to stop it from entering their domain and causing harm.

Maybe they used it for food, too.

Then the ants would carry the dying bee down into the hole; how he would love to see what happened down inside the nest. Maybe he could talk his mum round on the ant farm that he wants for his birthday, even though she hates bugs.

Stupid cow.

His mum is too scared of stupid things like that, and she is always fussing over everything.

Jacob is too engrossed in insect exploration—and exploitation—that he is completely oblivious to the hole in the dirt of the towpath. The front tyre sticks instantly, sending the rear half of the bike, Jacob, and his sweets up and over.

In a blur of blue skies, brown dirt and a spectrum of fifty-pence-worth of sweets, Jacob skids along the path, skinning his palms, elbows, and chin, and bloodying his nose.

A few seconds pass before the pain hits him.

Tears instantly well up in his eyes; he pushes himself up off the ground, and the moment he sees red, they burst their dam.

Big fat tears that twinkle in the sun form rivers through the dust on his cheeks as the first gut-wrenching sob bubbles out.

Once the first is unleashed, the rest come in waves as Jacob sits crying into his grazed hands.

"Alright, mate, what have you done, eh?"

A voice nearby makes him sniff back snot; he attempts to stop weeping.

A man in dirty black boots steps off the bottom step of a path leading up to the roadside.

"Come off your bike, have you? Oh, no—that's no good, is it?" The stranger crouches down to his level. "Let's have a look at you."

Jacob reluctantly shows the man his nose, chin, and bloodied palms.

He smells funny, not funny in a bad way. The smell makes him think of the multi-coloured sweets his gran used to eat, the ones with the man on the tin made out of sweets. Bertie Bassett. She openly admits that's who she named his dad after, even though his dad always denies it.

The man sucks air through his teeth. "Blimey O'Riley, you've got some good 'uns there, kid. Bet you've skinned your knees, too?"

The man stands up and casts an eye at his bike. "Your bike chain's off and the reflector's broken, too, but I can soon fix that—come on." With that, the man grabs Jacob's bike by the crossbar and lifts it.

Slowly, Jacob gets to his feet, wincing at his grazed knees. He knows all the protocols regarding walking off with strangers but he figures the man is just going to carry his bike up to the road and stick the chain back on for him.

The man doesn't turn back or offer assistance as he climbs the brick steps to the pavement.

He doesn't stop at the top of the steps, just walks into a driveway of a house directly beside the footpath's entrance.

Jacob stops outside the property's front garden, holding on to the black railed fence.

Intricate daffodils and other flowers of purple and blue are crafted into the metalwork. Even though he isn't interested in flowers, he does marvel at how something so detailed can be made of metal.

The man crunches across the loose gravel driveway and flips open his garage door.

There is no car inside, from what Jacob can see, just a kind of workshop with tools everywhere.

"Come on then, mate, let's get them cuts sorted and then I'll fix up your bike." It is the first time the man has acknowledged him since standing by the canal.

Jacob hesitates, feeling guilty for some reason. "Err…excuse me, Mister, but my parents said I'm not supposed to go anywhere with strangers."

The man nods indifferently, "You're Bert Willis' boy, aren't you, Joshua? I drink down The Trough with him." He laughs at something that must be funny, and says, "He's rubbish at darts."

Jacob smiles and walks down the driveway, if he is one of his dad's drinking buddies he can't be that bad. "It's Jacob, by the way."

The man chuckles, shakes his head, "Ah, well, I got the first letter right! You can call me Dave or Derrick, but my name's Duncan, ha ha!"

Jacob frowns for a second before catching the joke, momentarily forgetting his injuries, relaxing a little. "How about Doris?"

Duncan stops with his hands on his hips and roars with laughter, "Not on yer Nelly, Smelly or I'll box yer ears for you!"

Jacob likes him. He has visions of his father enjoying a pint of beer with him, talking about sport or the news, or whatever it is that grown-ups talk about.

He resembles the famous swimmer with the same name off the telly, this somehow makes him even more familiar.

Duncan wipes a hand over his bald head and cocks a thumb to the black-painted front door. "Come on, let's go fix you up."

Jacob follows Duncan into his house through a beige hallway and into a powder-blue kitchen.

Duncan gestures to a stool which sits against a breakfast bar. "Sit down, I'll get my first aid kit. You can have that can of pop if you want."

Jacob says thank you and sits at the breakfast bar watching Duncan pull a green plastic box from a drawer.

"So, what were you up to today, then? Apart from tearing down the towpath like ruddy Evel Knievel?" Duncan dabs a bottle of disinfectant against some cotton wool balls and proceeds to clean the grazes on Jacob's knees.

Jacob winces but keeps the noise to a minimum. "Just going to see my friends."

Duncan nods and begins to dress Jacob's wounds. Jacob notices the familiar smell, sweet but medicinal, like a cough lozenge.

When he has finished with his hands and knees, he takes a look at his face. "Don't think your chin and nose are that bad, just need a clean. Your mum can check them when you get home."

After wiping Jacob's face, Duncan stands up, puts the first aid kit away and the discarded rubbish in the bin.

"You can bring that can in the garage if you like." He winks, and walks through a door that leads into the garage.

Jacob picks up the unopened drink and follows Duncan into the poorly-lit garage.

Duncan already has the bike turned upside down, rested on its handlebars and seat, in a clearing amongst tool cupboards, a workbench, and heaps of random junk.

He catches Jacob eyeing the amount of stuff in the garage and chuckles, "Don't like to throw stuff away if it can be fixed or made into something else."

Jacob spots at least three other children's bikes amongst the junk and wonders where Duncan's kids are today. He doesn't look that old but maybe his kids have grown up, moved out and gotten jobs. Jacob can't wait to grow up, he is going to work in a zoo. The insect house will be his section, showing kids and their parents things that will make their skin crawl.

He is about to ask Duncan where his kids are when the words freeze on his lips. Duncan stands beside his bike with a large hessian potato sack. "What's that for?" he says, unable to hide the tremor in his voice. Duncan lifts the sack, and, after frowning for a second, laughs.

"What's it for? Kneeling on. You daft lad, you didn't think I was gonna put you in it, did you? I ain't the ruddy child catcher, you know!"

Jacob laughs uneasily and jumps about a foot in the air as Duncan jokingly lunges for him with the sack. He instinctively ducks out of the way as Duncan throws the cloth sack at his face.

"See? You're too bloody quick for me anyhow, daft sod. Now, let's get your bike sorted." He ruffles Jacob's mousy hair and stoops to pick the sack up.

Jacob is just thinking that Duncan is pretty cool, like a crazy uncle, when he springs up from where he crouches and knocks him out with a punch so hard and so fast, he never even feels it.

2.

His right eye throbs and feels glued shut. It aches more than anything he's experienced in his short life, but the lump on the back of his head is worse.

Jacob doesn't know where he is, only that it is dark and very cold.

Wherever he is smells bad, like an old shed or coal bunker. The flooring beneath him is covered with a rough fabric similar to the cloth sack Duncan had joked about with.

Duncan.

The realisation that Duncan has done this to him makes his bladder instantly let go.

He sits up, hugs his knees to his chest as the warm urine seeps through his pants and Bermuda shorts.

The tears that come make his outburst by the canal seem like a teardrop in the desert.

A fumbling comes from his left; instant brightness makes him shield his eyes and curl into a tighter ball.

"You're awake, then?" It's Duncan. "I'll leave this here." He places something down behind Jacob. "I'll leave the light on a bit. Let you get used to your surroundings."

Fumbling once more, a door being shut, bolts slide across, and something heavy is dragged.

Jacob opens his eyes.

He is in a square room with white painted walls. The paint flakes off in giant patches and peels away like sunburnt skin.

Mould and mildew rise with the dampness from the floor, making the walls two-toned.

Old sacks and ancient grotty rugs are strewn over the cold concrete floor. In the corner of the small room is a metal-framed bed with a filthy striped mattress. Fleece blankets are piled on the bed. Slatted stairs lead upwards and across the small space. Other than the bed and a tin bucket, there is nothing else in the room.

For what feels like hours, he just sits there hugging his knees, rocking back and forth, crying. The room is cold and he knows he has to move. He wants his mum and dad, —hell, he even wants his big brother. He'd give anything to be in a scrap with Michael right now.

One of Michael's Chinese burns, the ones that leave marks, would be bliss compared to this.

What the hell does Duncan want?

Jacob gets to his feet and sits on the bed.

The fleece blankets are rough, scratchy, and covered in stains, but he is freezing.

Wet and cold, he wraps the blankets around himself and lays in the foetal position.

At some point, he must have fallen asleep because Duncan appears in front of him without Jacob seeing him come in.

Duncan stands holding a washing up bowl with a towel draped over his arm and a smile on his face.

"Please let me go," Jacob says, each word difficult to say with the tremble in his voice.

Duncan sits down on the bed with the bowl on his lap. "Let's get you cleaned up, can't have you going home stinking of piss, can we?"

Jacob shakes his head, he doesn't want to wash in front of this man, let alone allow him to do it for him.

"You'll do as you're told if you wanna go home. Now take your clothes off, I'll wash and dry them so your mum don't moan."

"Please, I don't want to," Jacob pleads.

Duncan shoots him a stern expression that says, *If you don't do it then I will, and you won't like it, believe you me.*

Jacob pushes the blankets back, reluctantly gets to his feet, and fumbles with the zipper of his top.

Duncan's expression glazes over when he watches his fingers shaking over the fastener.

He smiles slightly, grabs Jacob's lapels, and tears his jacket open. Jacob flinches at the sudden attack and once again the tears come.

"Don't be such a girl." The man reaches for something at the foot of the bed, something black and oblong like a ghetto blaster. He lays the thing on the ground and fiddles with some switches. A small four-inch square black-and-white TV screen flickers on.

He turns a dial; pictures come and go as he tunes through the stations.

...A cobbled street, wet with drizzle, appears on the mini television; music begins playing as the camera pans back and shows two children in raincoats splashing amongst the puddles...

The music starts, but Jacob already knows what is showing on the TV—the children are Jane and Johnny.

Music, twinkly music-box music, drowns out the patter of raindrops-on-cobbles as the camera pans backwards, up. The scene morphs into a brightly-drawn cartoon version, a happy cartoon man with thick glasses and curly hair chuckles at the playing children, closes his umbrella, smiles up at the camera in the sky…

Duncan pulls at Jacob's clothes and breathes heavily through his nose.

"Now you just watch the program while I clean you up."

Jacob pushes his hands out against Duncan's arms but the man cruelly shoves him down on the bed, one hand ripping at his clothes whilst the other forces his face to the side to watch the TV. Through bleary eyes, Jacob subconsciously takes in the familiar program. He doesn't watch it anymore; it is for babies. The man who is on it annoys him, some comedian his parents like, and is always joking about the puppet characters having strings. As Duncan yanks Jacob's trousers down, the man on the TV begins to spin and sing, *"Come, come with me, down Diamond Drive."*

When the man has done what he's done, he pulls up his crumpled trousers from around his ankles and runs up the stairs, each step in time with the beats of Jacob's heart.

The realisation that he probably won't be going home hits Jacob when Duncan leaves him, shivering, naked on the bed.

Duncan returns with a black bin bag and barely acknowledges him as he thrusts his torn clothing into the sack.

Jacob hugs his knees to his chest and stares through the funny little portable television. Words are said but he doesn't hear them. Duncan crouches down low, his liquorice-and-tobacco breath panting in his face.

"Get cleaned up."

He takes a sponge meant for dishes out of the lukewarm water in the bowl and pushes it into his face.

Jacob's hands move automatically, grasping the sodden material.

Duncan stands up and throws his t-shirt to him. "Put that on, I'll get you some real clothes later."

Later.

It is the first word that properly registers with Jacob, *later*. Funny how such a word can bestow both equal amounts of hope and horror.

Later.

He spends the first night huddled naked against the wall beneath stinking, scratchy blankets, Duncan's t-shirt discarded on the floor.

Duncan never comes back down into the cellar that day and Jacob has only moved once to scrub himself down with the sponge and the cold water.

His skin is raw from using the harsh green side of the washing-up sponge. He needs to get rid of the smell of him, and the stuff that came out of him, out of his thing when he touched him.

Fresh tears resurface when he thinks about Duncan's rough, calloused hands touching him everywhere, his hot breath and wet kisses as he pressed his face all over him.

It is wrong what he did; they taught them at school that you mustn't go anywhere with strangers, never to take sweets off them, either. But they never told you why you mustn't, they never told you they would hurt you. They never told you they would do things to you. They never told you they would do the things Duncan has done.

He doesn't know what he thought the strangers *would* do, maybe take you away and you would never see your mum and dad again.

Before, he had visions of hundreds of taken children working in some factory that went on forever whilst cackling strangers towered over them, eating sweets they would never share.

He never thought they would do the things Duncan has done, he didn't even understand what or why he had done it, only that it hurt.

Jacob wonders if this is how the bee feels in the spider's web, but that always seemed to be over so much sooner.

The next day it happens again.

At the same time.

Duncan switches the TV on at the same time as that children's program.

This time Jacob kicks and screams; this time it is worse, a lot worse.

This time it hurts.

This time there's blood.

Afterwards, as he lays crying and bleeding, Duncan tries to be nice, tells him he is sorry and that he will be going soon, that it will all be over.

"I'll make you a slap-up dinner before you go, eh?" Duncan says, looking down sadly at him. He pats his bare legs, points to the fresh bowl of water, and runs up the stairs.

Jacob waits until he hears the bolt slide across and the heavy object being dragged across the doorway before he grabs the washing-up sponge.

Jacob wraps himself in the stinking blanket, the coarse material irritating the scratches and grazes on his skin. Even though he hasn't eaten in two days, the thought of Duncan returning with food makes him feel sick.

Maybe if he doesn't eat he will get ill and have to be taken to the doctors.

Or maybe he will die.

He doesn't know how long he has been huddled thinking about his own death. Thinking about death for the first time in his short life.

Duncan leaves the portable TV on; the children's programs have finished and the news is on.

The sound of grating against the stone floor tells him it's dinner time.

The bolts are shot back and he listens as the cellar door is opened and Duncan's footsteps fall on the wooden steps above his head. He peers through the slats at the man's bare ankles as he descends, sending a fine powder of dust raining down onto his bed.

The waft of greasy cooking comes from above.

"Here," Duncan calls cheerfully, stopping on one of the steps, "made you my special fry-up."

A high-pitched klaxon rings from the house above and Jacob watches as Duncan is physically startled. The stairs creak where he spins towards the source of the calamitous noise.

A string of barely decipherable curses fly from his mouth as he loses his balance and comes crashing down the stairs.

Jacob sits up wide-eyed as he hears the man tumble down the steps. He expects further cursing, anger, but all he can hear is the constant ringing from above.

Jacob gets off the bed and slowly walks out of the nook he is in. A tray lies on the floor, a smashed plate with egg-mush, sausages and chips surrounds Duncan's hand. Jacob stares at that hand, waiting for it to twitch, but it doesn't. Duncan lies at the foot of the steps, half-naked, a small pool of blood around his head, eyes closed. Jacob shuffles closer and steps over him, half-expecting his hand to clamp around his ankle. The stairs loom ahead, heart thudding in his chest he starts to climb them.

Duncan's groans begin almost as soon as he places a foot on the first step.

Jacob whimpers and turns to see Duncan regaining consciousness.

He races up the steps towards a flaking cream door.

"No," Duncan manages to shout as Jacob reaches out towards the brass door handle. Jacob runs towards the persistent wailing noise.

"Wait," Duncan pleads as Jacob opens the door. He takes a glimpse over his shoulder: Duncan is scrabbling up the steps on all fours, his face full of teeth and red fury.

Jacob slams the door shut and pushes the three heavy bolts across. They are rusted and stiff; the iron tears at the skin of his palms, but he doesn't care.

Black smoke fills the room he is in, a green light flashes in time with the shrill noise.

A smoke alarm.

A white rectangle of light shines through the thick air, the outline of a door. Jacob runs at it as quickly as he can. The door crashes open and he falls onto Duncan's driveway, the evening sun blinding him as he rolls across the brickwork.

The intake of smoke has been enough to tighten his throat and no sound will come from his mouth when he tries to shout. He coughs, splutters, a thin mixture of bile burns its way onto the ground, and Jacob finds his voice.

He screams.

3.

The big woman comes bungling out of the house opposite.

He doesn't know the woman from Adam, that is one of his mother's sayings, and the woman is definitely a mum.

She is huge, with massive, white, doughy arms and breasts that are barely contained beneath a pink vest top. She kicks off cheap flip-flops, her shrink-wrapped, tree-trunk legs wobbling with the sudden bout of unfamiliar exertion. "George!" she shrieks out at the top of her raucous voice, "call an ambulance!"

She falls to her knees and scoops Jacob up, cradling him to her epic bosom. Tears fall from deep-set eyes over pudgy cheeks as she looks down at him and whimpers, "Oh, dear Lord."

Jacob lets himself be coddled like a baby; to him, she is a vision of angelic perfection.

4.

It isn't until he has finished bawling in her arms and hears the sound of sirens that the lady notices the furls of smoke curling from around the door he has come through. Fresh fear washes her troubled face as she sees the first flicker of flames against the window panes.

Jacob watches, transfixed, as the interior of the ground floor fills with smoke and spits out fire.

"Oh my god, is Duncan still inside?" The woman lifts him to his feet and moves away from the house.

The sirens are getting closer. A scrawny man with long grey hair comes running down the driveway opposite, in just a pair of shorts.

"The bloody house is on fire!" he says, before waving his hands above his head at the rapidly approaching ambulance.

The lady sits Jacob down on the grass kerbside, puts her arm around him, and promises him everything will be alright.

"Love, were you in there on your own? Do you know if Duncan is inside the house?" she repeats, pointing at the burning building.

Jacob flinches as the heat from inside shatters the windows and the thick black smoke billows out into the summer sky.

He doesn't say a word.

Matthew Cash

*Tempted by the voices,
which harshly curse me inside,
that force through images most foul,
to the point where I can feel you touching me,
Despite this life, I know that a part of me died.*

Matthew Cash

The Beginning.

It is when the police take him away in their car that Jacob sees himself staring out of a poster pinned to a tree. The picture is from the previous Christmas; he'd gotten the Millennium Falcon. Below his photo was the word MISSING.

All the policeman had said, when he had told him what his name was, was that he would be alright now, that he would radio someone to go and fetch his mum and dad.

At the police station, they give him some clothes and take the blanket off him for evidence. He is given squash and a sandwich but finds it difficult to eat; a massive knot that he would later learn to be anxiety clenches his stomach as if it is in a tight fist. He starts crying again when his mother bursts into the room, her eyes streaming with continuous tears. His dad, not normally one to show many emotions, is equally moved.

He falls into his mother's arms and welcomes her wet kisses.

"Now, I know this might be very difficult for you Jacob, but we really need to know what happened, why you were in that house," a young policeman asks. His mum squeezes his hand and his dad takes a slow sip of his plastic cup of coffee.

Jacob tells them all what happened, everything.

As a rule, he is very good at remembering, not that there is any chance of forgetting his ordeal.

He uses the only words he knows how to describe the things that man did to him, and when he can't find the right ones, he shows them in gestures like on that program his parents watch, *Give Us a Clue*. Whilst he describes everything that has happened, the policeman writes it down in his notebook.

His mum and dad are silent throughout the interview, as instructed by the policeman, but as soon as it is over, his mum bursts into fresh tears whilst his dad paces about the room with his fists clenched.

Afterwards, he is taken away with his mum and a special nurse, for some tests. Tests that the nurse and his mum keep telling him are important. Meanwhile, the policeman has a word with his dad.

He whines and protests but feels safe because his mum is with him. The nurse takes blood from his arm and does a few funny things he doesn't really understand, but afterwards, she gives him sweets.

6.

It is as if he has been swapped with a completely different brother but still looks exactly the same.

Once, on BBC 2, there had been a cool film about aliens that made copies of everyone on earth in big pea pods. It reminds Jacob of that, the few days since he came back home. Michael is being nice to him for the first time in ages. But that night, it seems his brother is trying to disguise being upset.

"What's the matter, Mikey?" Jacob asks, watching his brother reading on his bed.

"Nothing much, Jake, just them pair arguing downstairs. Come on, let's go to sleep, back at school tomorrow." Michael slams his book shut and switches off the bedside lamp.

Jacob wonders what his mum and dad were fighting about. They never really argue, at least not loud enough for them to hear, and not at night time.

Guilt that it is somehow his fault bubbles up; he can't sleep.

When Michael's peaceful snores sound, Jacob whips back the cover on his bed and creeps to the bedroom door.

Before he was taken, Michael would have woken up, stuck his leg out between his bed and the chest of drawers, stopping him from leaving the room and bothering their parents.

He did that the first night he came home, and it made him shriek that much, their dad had come in and whacked Michael.

Jacob treads carefully down the thickly-carpeted stairs outside his room, his parents' voices becoming clearer.

"...upping sticks, though," he hears his mother whine.

"Yeah, I know, but what do you expect? At least it's not you that has to give up the best fucking job you've ever had!"

"Oh, I know, but it's just so far away, how we're not allowed to come back until that bastard is caught."

"Love, Jakey locked him inside a burning building," his father says, then his voice softens, "I know both of us wished the cunt had died in that fire but the fact is, he didn't."

Jacob feels a shiver run down his back, that means Duncan is still out there.

"Do you think he'll want to get him again?" his mother says, a tremble on her lips.

"Babe, I don't know how these monsters' minds work, I'm not sure I want to, but it's not worth the risk, we both know that. Once the police have banged him up, who knows? We could come back."

His parents' voices quieten and change into gentle sobbing.

We have to go away, that's what they are talking about.

Jacob sits on the step and picks at the line where two strips of wallpaper meet.

We will have to go far away, from our granddads, grandmas, aunts, uncles, cousins, far away from the place we all love and call home, and it is all his fault.

Jacob wishes he'd died in the fire, he and Duncan.

Matthew Cash

This fear and pain will not fade,
cannot believe that your body died,
because you're here, existing in my head,
without a body, your frightful spirit stayed.

"*He did, indeed, have an afterlife and he lived it in my head.*"
Dennis Nilsen

Foreword / Afterword

A few years back I got the idea of writing a backwards ghost story, taking the basic principle of the reader not finding out who the ghost is until the very end of the book, or the actual 'ghost' coming into its non-corporeal form at the end.

The problem is that I don't cope with ghost stories very well, reading them or writing them.

As a reader, I find them unbelievable, even though I have a great fascination with the subject in real life. I can never fully commit to a ghost story and there's always an element of indifference in me when I read them.

Out of the ghost stories I've read and loved there has to be something more to it for me to get to the final page and be completely satisfied.

I have read many wonderful, well-written ghost stories that have been ruined by the very end.

In my eyes, it's one of the hardest sub-genres to get right, and few have passed my overall seal of approval.

Two examples that I can think of to hand, but there are more, are a film and a book.

The film *Ghost Stories*, starring Paul Whitehouse and co-written by a great writer, Jeremy Dyson, ticked all the right boxes for me.

The book is Adam Nevill's *No One Gets Out Alive*.

This book is as depressing as hell and I honestly didn't think I'd finish it but 2020 has been as depressing as hell, too.

In November/December I found I could tap into that and get it out of my system in ways other than overeating and worrying about England being a prison island with a mutated strain of Coronavirus running amok.

Maybe after this, if my mood changes, I'll be able to write something more light-hearted or at least more bloodthirsty.

That's if I'm not having to stop people from trying to snatch my children for food.

Thank you for reading, and I hope to be back again soon.

Matty-Bob
XXXX
Very high risk,
Tier 3,
England.

About Matthew Cash

Matthew Cash, or Matty-Bob Cash as he is known to most, was born and raised in Suffolk, which is the setting for his debut novel *Pinprick*.

He is compiler and editor of *Death by Chocolate*, a chocoholic horror anthology and the *12Days: STOCKING FILLERS* anthology.

In 2016, he launched his own publishing house, Burdizzo Books, and took shit-hot editor and author Em Dehaney on board to keep him in shape, and together they brought into existence *SPARKS*: an electrical horror anthology, *The Reverend Burdizzo's Hymn Book, Under the Weather*, Visions from the Void ***, and *The Burdizzo Mix Tape Vol. 1.* He has numerous solo releases on Kindle and several collections in paperback.

Originally, with Burdizzo Books, the intention was to compile charity anthologies a few times a year but his creation has grown into something so much more powerful *insert mad laughter here*.

He is currently working on numerous projects; his third novel, *FUR,* was launched in 2018.

*With *Back Road Books*
** With Jonathan Butcher

He has been writing stories since he first learned to write and most, although not all, tend to slip into the multi-layered murky depths of the horror genre.

His influences (from when he first started reading to present-day) are, to name but a small, select few: Roald Dahl, James Herbert, Clive Barker, Stephen King, Stephen Laws, and more recently, he enjoys Adam Nevill, F.R Tallis, Michael Bray, Gary Fry, William Meikle and Iain Rob Wright (who featured Matty-Bob in his famous *A-Z of Horror* title *M is For Matty-Bob*, plus Matthew wrote his version of events, which was included as a bonus). He is a father of two, a husband of one, and a zookeeper of numerous fur babies.

You can find him here:
www.facebook.com/pinprickbymatthewcash
https://www.amazon.co.uk/-/e/B010MQTWKK
www.burdizzobooks.com

Other Releases by Matthew Cash

Novels:

Virgin and The Hunter
Pinprick
FUR

Novellas:

Ankle Biters
KrackerJack
Illness
Clinton Reed's FAT
Hell And Sebastian
Waiting for Godfrey
Deadbeard
The Cat Came Back
KrackerJack 2
Demon Thingy [with Jonathan Butcher]
Werwolf
Frosty
Keida-in-the-flames
Tesco a-go-go

Short Stories

Why Can't I Be You?
Slugs and Snails and Puppydog Tails
Oldtimers
Hunt The C*nt

Anthologies compiled and edited by Matthew Cash:

Death by Chocolate
12 Days: STOCKING FILLERS
12 Days: 2016 Anthology
12 Days: 2017 [with Em Dehaney]
The Reverend Burdizzo's Hymn Book (with Em Dehaney)
Sparks [with Em Dehaney]
Visions from the Void [with Jonathan Butcher]
Under the Weather
Welcome to a town called Hell
Burdizzo Mix Tape Volume 1
Corona-Nation Street
Beneath the Leaves

Anthologies Featuring Matthew Cash

Rejected for Content 3: Vicious Vengeance
JEApers Creepers
Full Moon Slaughter
Down the Rabbit Hole: Tales of Insanity

Collections
The Cash Compendium Volume 1
The Cash Compendium Continuity

Websites:
www.Facebook.com/pinprickbymatthewcash

www.burdizzobooks.com

Pinprick
Matthew Cash

All villages have their secrets, and Brantham is no different.

Twenty years ago, after foolish risk-taking turned into tragedy, Shane left the rural community under a cloud of suspicion and rumour. Events from that night remained unexplained, memories erased, questions unanswered. Now a notorious politician, he returns to his birthplace when the offer from a property developer is too good to decline.

With big plans to haul Brantham into the 21st century, the developers have already made a devastating impact on the once-quaint village.

But then the headaches begin, followed by the nightmarish visions.

Soon Shane wishes he had never returned, as Brantham reveals its ugly secret.

Virgin and The Hunter
Matthew Cash

Hi, I'm God. And I have a confession to make.

I live with my two best friends and the girl of my dreams, Persephone. When the opportunity knocks, we are usually down the pub having a few drinks, or we'll hang out in Christchurch Park until it gets dark, then go home to do college stuff. Even though I struggle a bit financially, life is good, carefree.

Well, it was.

Things have started going downhill recently, from the moment I started killing people.

KrackerJack
Matthew Cash

Five people wake up in a warehouse, bound to chairs. Before each of them, tacked to the wall are their witness testimonies.

They each played a part in labelling one of Britain's most loved family entertainers a paedophile and sex offender.

Clearly, revenge is the reason they have been brought here, but the man they accused is supposed to be dead.

Opportunity knocks and Diddy Dave Diamond has one last game show to host—and it's a knockout.

Krackerjack2
Matthew Cash

Ever wondered what would happen if a celebrity faked their own death and decided they had changed their minds?

Two years ago, publicly-shunned comedian Diddy Dave Diamond convinced the nation that he was dead, only to return from beyond the grave to seek retribution on those who ruined his career and tainted his legacy.

Innocent or not, only one person survived Diddy Dave Diamond's last-ever game show, but the forfeit prize was imprisonment for similar alleged crimes.

Prison is not kind to inmates with those types of convictions, as the sole survivor finds out, but there's a sudden glimmer of hope.

Someone has surfaced in the public eye, claiming to be the dead comedian.

Fur
Matthew Cash

The old-aged pensioners of Boxford are set in their ways, loyal to each other and their daily routines. With families and loved ones either moved on to pastures new or maybe even the next life, these folks can become dependent on one another.

But what happens when the natural ailments of old age begin to take their toll? What if they were given the opportunity to heal and overcome the things that make everyday life less tolerable? What if they were given this ability without their consent?

When a group of local thugs attack the village's wealthy Victor Krauss, they unwittingly create a maelstrom of events that not only could destroy their home but everyone in and around it.

Are the old folk the cause or the cure of the horrors?

Also from
Burdizzo Books:

The Children at The Bottom of The Gardden
Jonathan Butcher

At the edge of the coastal city of Seadon, there stands a dilapidated farmhouse, and at the back of the farmhouse there is a crowd of rotten trees, where something titters and calls.

The Gardden.

Its playful voice promises games, magic, wonders, lies – and roaring torrents of blood.

It speaks not just to its eccentric keeper, Thomas, but also to the outcasts and deviants from Seadon's criminal underworld.

At first, they are too distracted by their own tangled mistakes and violent lives to notice, but one-by-one they'll come: a restless Goth, a cheating waster, a sullen concubine, a perverted drug baron, and a murderous sociopath.

Haunted by shadowed things with coal-black eyes, something malicious and ancient will lure them ever-closer. And on a summer's day not long from now, they'll gather beneath the leaves in a place where nightmares become flesh, secrets rise up from the dark, and a voice coaxes them to play and stay, yes, yes, yes, forever.

The Little Exorcist
Alys Daddi

Molly's dad, Wayne, has always been a practical joker, a proper wind-up merchant, his sense of humour holds no bounds, and when what he thinks is a trick at his expense backfires, he is left feeling unusual.

Wayne's silliness stoops to new and more juvenile levels but strangely, he professes to having no recollection of this behaviour.

Things go from silly to strange when these events turn into regular blackouts and Wayne reveals secrets from his past that may have implications on his present-day mental health. With his family and friends trying to support him and come to terms with living with someone who may have Dissociative Identity or Multiple Personality Disorder, it's only his daughter Molly who wonders if there is more to his illness than the psychiatric team can deal with.

The Wassailers
Em Dehaney

This wickedly sinister Christmas poem by Em Dehaney is a traditional folk tale with a terrifying twist, warning of the dangers of modern greed and consumerism. Featuring pen-and-ink illustrations by Krzysztof Wroński that are dark, dense and dripping with old-world menace.

Burdizzo Books have brought the two together, along with a foreword by no other than the master of horror Graham Masterton, in this gruesome, yet gripping, unique festive nightmare.

Curl up by the fire, fill your cup with mulled wine, and pray The Wassailers don't knock on your door.

Printed in Great Britain
by Amazon